W9-CPP-613

Also by Stuart Gibbs

The FunJungle series
Belly Up
Poached
Big Game
Panda-monium
Lion Down
Tyrannosaurus Wrecks
Bear Bottom
Whale Done

The Spy School series
Spy School
Spy Camp
Evil Spy School
Spy Ski School
Spy School Secret Service
Spy School Goes South
Spy School British Invasion
Spy School Revolution
Spy School at Sea
Spy School Project X

Spy School the Graphic Novel
(with Anjan Sarkar)

The Moon Base Alpha series
Space Case
Spaced Out
Waste of Space

The Charlie Thorne series
Charlie Thorne and the Last Equation
Charlie Thorne and the Lost City
Charlie Thorne and the Curse of Cleopatra

The Once Upon a Tim series
Once Upon a Tim
The Labyrinth of Doom

The Last Musketeer

STUART GIBBS

ILLUSTRATED BY ANJAN SARKAR

spy camp

THE GRAPHIC NOVEL

A **spy school** NOVEL

Simon & Schuster Books for Young Readers
New York London Toronto Sydney New Delhi

SIMON & SCHUSTER BOOKS FOR YOUNG READERS
An imprint of Simon & Schuster Children's Publishing Division
1230 Avenue of the Americas, New York, New York 10020
This book is a work of fiction. Any references to historical events,
real people, or real places are used fictitiously. Other names, characters,
places, and events are products of the author's imagination, and any resemblance
to actual events or places or persons, living or dead, is entirely coincidental.

Adapted from *Spy Camp* (2013) by Stuart Gibbs

Interior design by Lucy Ruth Cummins
The text for this book was set in Memphis LT Std.
The illustrations for this book were rendered digitally.
Manufactured in China
1122 SCP
First Edition
10 9 8 7 6 5 4 3 2 1
Library of Congress Cataloging-in-Publication Data
Names: Gibbs, Stuart, 1969– author. | Sarkar, Anjan, illustrator.
Title: Spy camp the graphic novel / Stuart Gibbs ; illustrated by Anjan Sarkar.
Description: First Simon & Schuster Books for Young Readers hardcover edition. |
New York : Simon & Schuster Books for Young Readers, 2023. |
Series: Spy school | Audience: Ages 8–12 | Audience: Grades 4–6 |
Summary: "Top-secret training continues into summer for aspiring spy Ben Ripley—
and so does the danger"— Provided by publisher.
Identifiers: LCCN 2021055680 (print) | LCCN 2021055681 (ebook) |
ISBN 9781534499386 (hardcover) | ISBN 9781534499379 (paperback) |
ISBN 9781534499393 (ebook)
Subjects: CYAC: Graphic novels. | Spies—Fiction. | Schools—Fiction. |
LCGFT: Spy comics. | Graphic novels.
Classification: LCC PZ7.7.G5324 Sp 2023 (print) | LCC PZ7.7.G5324 (ebook) |
DDC 741.5/973—dc23/eng/20211124
LC record available at https://lccn.loc.gov/2021055680
LC ebook record available at https://lccn.loc.gov/2021055681

For Ciara —S. G.

For Kenji —A. S.

HIGHLY
CLASSIFIED

FOR YOUR EYES ONLY

DESTROY
AFTER
READING

If you read this
without permission, you're in
BIG TROUBLE!

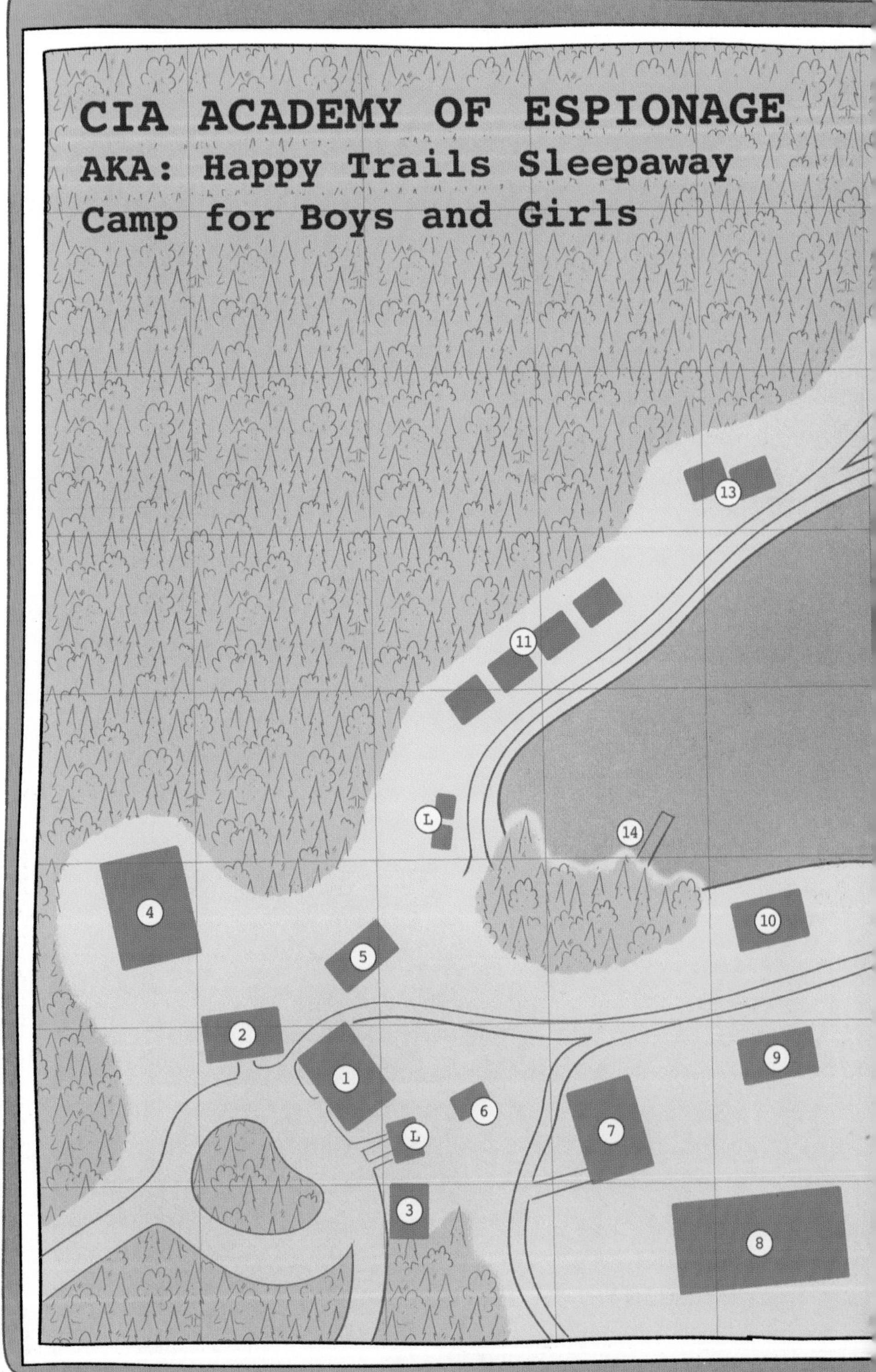
CIA ACADEMY OF ESPIONAGE
AKA: Happy Trails Sleepaway
Camp for Boys and Girls
1
2
3
4
5
6
7
8
9
10
11
13
14
L
L

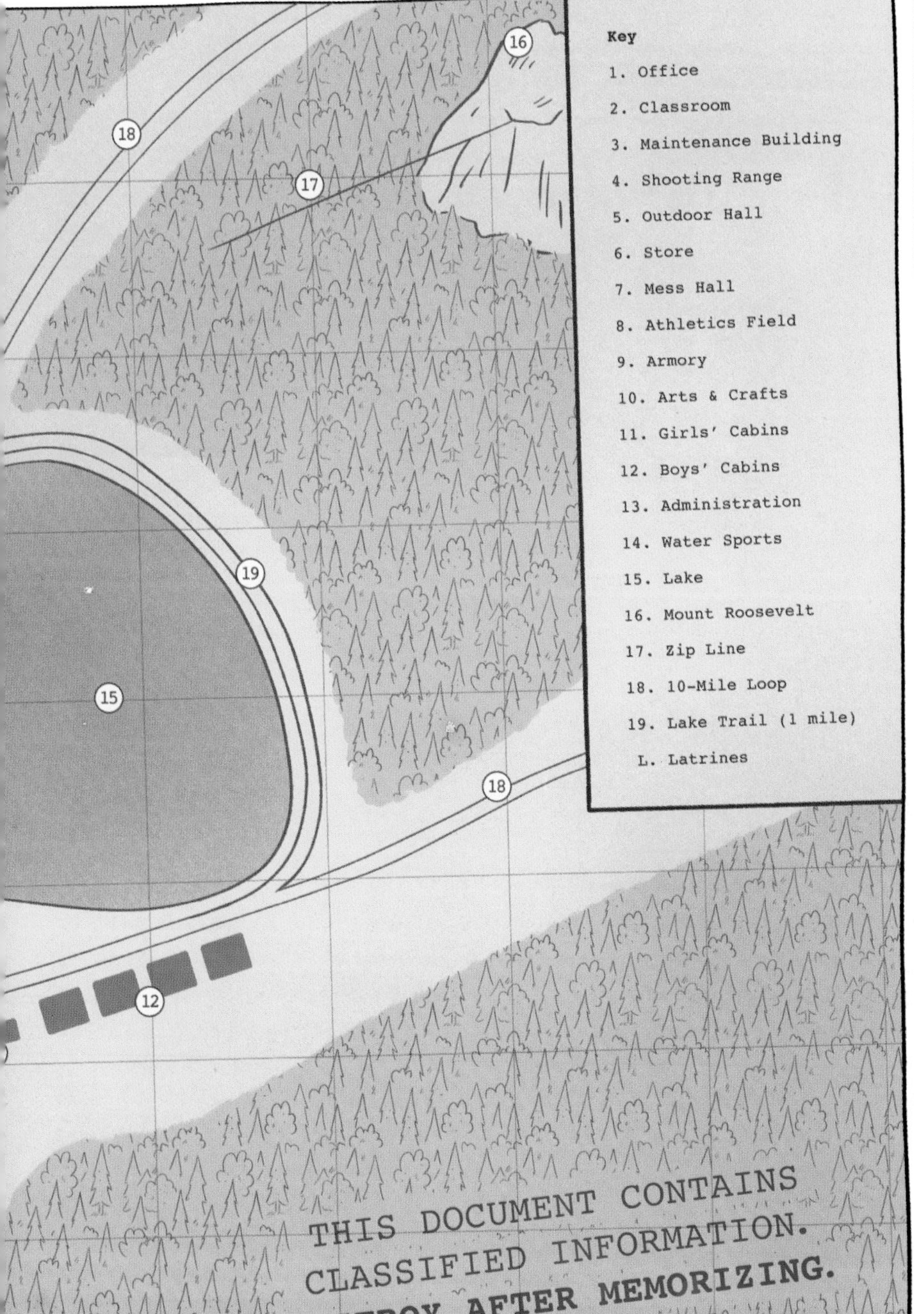
16
18
17
19
15
18
12
Key
1. Office
2. Classroom
3. Maintenance Building
4. Shooting Range
5. Outdoor Hall
6. Store
7. Mess Hall
8. Athletics Field
9. Armory
10. Arts & Crafts
11. Girls' Cabins
12. Boys' Cabins
13. Administration
14. Water Sports
15. Lake
16. Mount Roosevelt
17. Zip Line
18. 10-Mile Loop
19. Lake Trail (1 mile)
L. Latrines
THIS DOCUMENT CONTAINS
CLASSIFIED INFORMATION.
DESTROY AFTER MEMORIZING.

Name: Benjamin Ripley

Age: 12 (but about to turn 13)

Year at the academy: First

Code name: Smokescreen

Mental acuity: Very intelligent. Level 16 math skills.

Physical acuity: Very little. Hopeless when it comes to weaponry. DO NOT let him have a weapon under any circumstances. It would be wise to not even let him use a fork in the mess hall.

Recruited to the Academy of Espionage five months ago as part of Operation Creeping Badger.

Although Ripley was secretely brought in as bait to lure a mole out of hiding, due to several unforeseen events, he wound up playing a larger role in the operation than originally expected.

As a result, he is the only person at the CIA to have ever had direct contact with the nefarious evil organization known as SPYDER. In fact, SPYDER actually tried to recruit him, although he turned them down.

Because Ripley started at the academy late in the year, he is a bit behind other students in his class and still may not be fully informed of all academy practices.

UNDER ARREST

Name: Murray Hill

Age: 13

Year at the academy: No longer valid

Code name: Washout

Mental acuity: Not bad; very sneaky and underhanded

Physical ability: Embarrassing

Murray Hill flunked his first year at the academy and then spent much of his second year working as a covert mole for SPYDER. Thanks to Operation Creeping Badger, he was apprehended before he could blow up the academy and has now been incarcerated at the Apple Valley Reformation Camp for Delinquent Teens.

Name: Erica Hale

Age: 15

Year at the academy: Third

Code name: Ice Queen

Mental acuity: Excellent

Physical acuity: Off the charts

Despite merely being a third-year student, Hale is easily the best student at the academy. This can be attributed, in part, to the fact that she is a legacy: The Hale family can be traced back to Nathan and Elias Hale, spies for the Colonial forces during the American Revolution. Thus, the Hales have been spying for the United States since before there was a United States.

Erica is adept in five forms of martial arts, can speak six languages and has familiarity with a great variety of weapons. However, her interpersonal skills are somewhat lacking. She is regarded by her fellow students (and much of the faculty) as cold, impersonal, and kind of scary.

She was integral to the success of Operation Creeping Badger despite the fact that she was not supposed to be a part of that operation at all.

Name: Agent Alexander Hale

Age: Classified

Code names: Gray Wolf, Alpha Dog, Blazing Stallion, Vengeful Lion

Alexander Hale has been a highly decorated agent for many years at the CIA and has served on dozens of operations in exotic locales around the world. He comes from a long line of agents and is the father of agent-in-training Erica Hale.

According to his most recent reports, he was integral to the defeat of SPYDER in Operation Creeping Badger.

Zoe Zibbell, first year

Warren Reeves, first year

Chip Schacter, fourth year

The Principal
(name withheld)

Tina Cuevo, graduate
Jawa O'Shea, second year
Hank Schacter, seventh year
Claire Hutchins,
exchange student,
British MI6

From:
Office of CIA Internal Investigations
CIA Headquarters
Langley, Virginia

To:
[REDACTED]
Director of Covert Affairs
The White House
Washington, DC

Classified Documents Enclosed
Security Level AA2
For Your Eyes Only

Well, here we go again.

As you are probably aware, the events of June 10–16 of this year, in which [REDACTED] have warranted a significant internal investigation. Once again, Mr. Benjamin Ripley, aka Smokescreen, a first-year student at the Academy of Espionage, was involved. The following pages are compiled from 54 hours of debriefings.

This episode, although not an official CIA operation at the time, is currently being classified as Operation Angry Jackal. The events described indicate a disturbing trend of [REDACTED] and [REDACTED] If Mr. Ripley and the others involved are to be believed, we came perilously close to [REDACTED]

After these documents have been read, they are to be destroyed immediately, in accordance with CIA Security Directive 163-12A. No discussion of these pages will be tolerated, except during the review, which will be conducted in a secure location at [REDACTED] Please note that no weapons will be allowed at said meeting.

I look forward to hearing your thoughts.

[REDACTED]
Director of Internal Investigations

Cc:
[REDACTED]
[REDACTED]
[REDACTED]
[REDACTED]

NOW THAT EXAMS ARE FINISHED, ALL I WANT IS A HOME-COOKED MEAL. THE CAFETERIA HERE DOESN'T CUT IT.

YOU MEAN ST. SMITHEN'S SCIENCE ACADEMY DOESN'T SPECIALIZE IN FINE DINING?

NO. I THINK THEY SERVE US THE SCIENCE EXPERIMENTS THAT HAVE GONE HORRIBLY WRONG.

KNOW WHAT I'M EXCITED FOR? YOUR BIRTHDAY'S COMING UP! YOUR PARTY'S STILL A GO, RIGHT?

YEAH. MY PARENTS RENTED THE REC ROOM AT FUNLAND FOR A FEW HOURS.
COOL! SPEAKING OF WHICH, MY BROTHER SAID HE COULD GET US SUMMER JOBS THERE. DOING ARCADE MAINTENANCE.

WHICH MEANS WE'D BASICALLY GET PAID TO PLAY VIDEO GAMES ALL DAY.
WHAT DO YOU SAY?

SOUNDS PERFECT.
NICE AND SAFE.

SAFE?

I MEANT EASY.
I'M LOOKING FORWARD TO A NICE, RELAXING SUMMER BREAK.
TOXIN RESISTANCE WORKSHOP
WITH BLAKE DIAMOND

ME TOO. THIS IS GOING TO BE THE BEST SUMMER EVER!
BOMB CLUB
MISSING SNAKE

423

UH, MIKE? I GOTTA GO.

Benjamin—
Come see me at once.
—the Principal

HEY, SMOKESCREEN! WE NEED ONE MORE FOR SOCCER. ARE YOU IN?
SORRY. THE PRINCIPAL WANTS TO SEE ME.
IS SOMETHING WRONG?
I HOPE NOT.
WELL, IF YOU FEEL LIKE IT, COME FIND US AFTERWARD! WE COULD USE ANOTHER STRIKER.

PLEASE STATE YOUR NAME, RANK, AND BUSINESS.

PAT PAT!

BENJAMIN RIPLEY, FIRST-YEAR STUDENT. THE PRINCIPAL ASKED TO SEE ME.

MR. RIPLEY, MY SOURCES TELL ME YOU'RE PLANNING TO GO HOME FOR THE SUMMER.

SOURCES? WHAT SOURCES?

OH, THE USUAL. I'M SURE YOU'RE AWARE THAT WE KEEP CLOSE TABS ON OUR STUDENT BODY HERE. LISTENING DEVICES, PHONE TAPS, THAT SORT OF THING.

YOU'RE TAPPING MY PHONE?
Ripley:
Now that exams are finished, all I want is a home-cooked meal. The cafeteria here doesn't cut it.
Caller:
You mean St. Smithen's Science Academy doesn't specialize in fine dining?
Ripley:
No. I think they serve us the science experiments that have gone horribly wrong.
Caller:

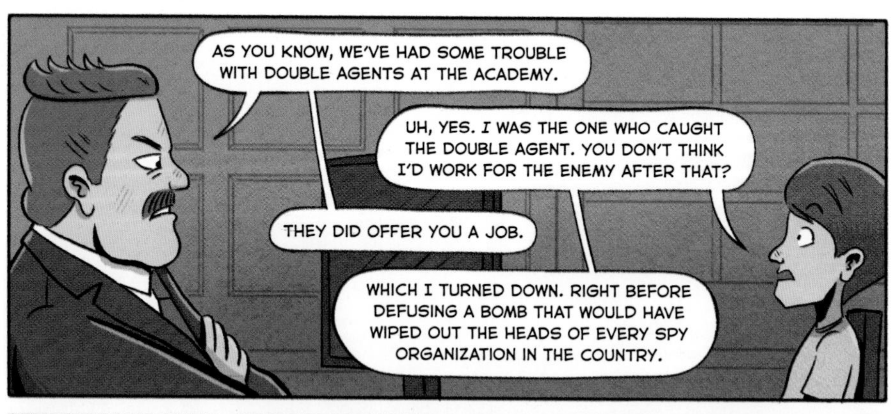
AS YOU KNOW, WE'VE HAD SOME TROUBLE WITH DOUBLE AGENTS AT THE ACADEMY.
UH, YES. *I* WAS THE ONE WHO CAUGHT THE DOUBLE AGENT. YOU DON'T THINK I'D WORK FOR THE ENEMY AFTER THAT?
THEY DID OFFER YOU A JOB.
WHICH I TURNED DOWN. RIGHT BEFORE DEFUSING A BOMB THAT WOULD HAVE WIPED OUT THE HEADS OF EVERY SPY ORGANIZATION IN THE COUNTRY.

THE POINT IS, I'D LIKE TO KNOW HOW YOU PLANNED TO AVOID SUMMER SCHOOL.

THE ACADEMY HAS A SUMMER SCHOOL?

OF COURSE. EVIL DOESN'T TAKE HOLIDAYS. WHY SHOULD WE?

NO ONE EVER TOLD ME THERE WAS SUMMER SCHOOL.

DON'T BE RIDICULOUS. EVERY NEW RECRUIT IS INFORMED ABOUT MANDATORY SUMMER EDUCATION DURING THE VERY FIRST ASSEMBLY OF THE SCHOOL YEAR.
SLIDE

I WASN'T AT THE FIRST ASSEMBLY. YOU DIDN'T RECRUIT ME UNTIL A FEW MONTHS AGO. IN JANUARY.

WELL, YOU SHOULD HAVE FIGURED IT OUT ANYHOW. YOU'RE STUDYING TO BE A SPY, FOR PETE'S SAKE. IT'S NOT LIKE THE SCHOOL'S EXISTENCE IS A SECRET.

THE SCHOOL'S EXISTENCE *IS* A SECRET.

I'VE HAD ENOUGH OF YOUR LIP! WOULD YOU LIKE TO BEGIN SUMMER SCHOOL ON PROBATION?
SLAM!

ALL THE OTHER STUDENTS HAVE BEEN PACKING THEIR THINGS. AREN'T THEY ATTENDING SUMMER SCHOOL TOO?
ABSOLUTELY. EVERYONE AT THE ACADEMY IS REQUIRED TO ATTEND SUMMER CLASSES. THEY'RE JUST NOT TAUGHT HERE.
THEN WHERE ARE THEY TAUGHT?

AT OUR WILDERNESS EDUCATION FACILITY.
?

WILDERNESS EDUCATION?

YES. PHYSICAL TRAINING AND SURVIVAL SKILLS. AFTER ALL, NINETY-NINE PERCENT OF THE WORLD IS OUTDOORS. A GOOD SPY NEEDS TO KNOW HOW TO GET ALONG THERE.

SO...IT'S KIND OF LIKE SPY CAMP.
IT'S NOT CAMP! IT'S AN ELITE WILDERNESS SURVIVAL TRAINING FACILITY. IT MERELY HAPPENS TO *LOOK* LIKE A CAMP.
SPIN!
AND AS FAR AS ANY OF YOUR FAMILY, FRIENDS, OR ANYONE ELSE KNOWS, YOU WILL BE ATTENDING A CAMP...

SADAM CAPTURED
THE HAPPY TRAILS SLEEPAWAY CAMP FOR BOYS AND GIRLS.

SHUFFLE!
SHUFFLE!

Your official transportation will be waiting for you at Union Station, Washington, DC, at 0700 hours Monday morning.
Bring a duffel bag, two pairs of pants, two pairs of shorts, seven pairs of underwear, seven shirts, seven pairs of socks, one pair of sturdy shoes, one thermal layer (top and bottom), one rain jacket, a bathing suit, a hat, sunblock, toiletries, a canteen, your standard-issue school survival kit, and snacks for the ride. DO NOT BRING WEAPONS. Those will be provided to you upon your arrival at Happy Trails.
Memorize the contents of this page, then destroy this document.

WHEN DOES IT START?
IN THREE DAYS. GO HOME, HAVE A NICE WEEKEND WITH YOUR FAMILY, AND THEN REPORT TO THE TRANSIT LOCATION ON MONDAY MORNING.

Ben

Hey, Ben!
Just wanted to let you know we'll be coming for you soon.
Your pals at SPYDER

FIRING RANGE, A FEW MINUTES LATER.

SWISH!

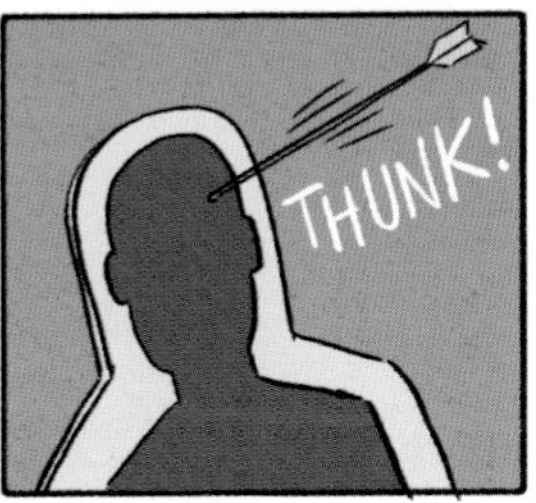
THUNK!

HOW WAS YOUR MEETING WITH THE PRINCIPAL?
HOW DID YOU KNOW ABOUT THAT?
I'M STUDYING TO BE A SPY. IT'S MY JOB TO KNOW THINGS.

I FOUND THIS IN MY ROOM JUST NOW.

LET'S TALK SOMEWHERE QUIETER.

CHEMICAL
AND BIOLOGICAL
WARFARE

HOT BEVERAGE

BEEP
BEEP!
A2
B2
B3
C2
C3
D2
D3

RESTRICTED:
DO NOT ENTER
WITHOUT
AUTHORIZATION.

JUST LIKE YOU AND I ARE THE ONLY ONES WHO KNOW YOUR DAD IS A FRAUD WHO TOOK CREDIT FOR US DEFEATING MURRAY HILL?

FIND A CLUE?

THIS NOTE'S PRACTICALLY STERILE. IT'S NOT JUST THAT THERE AREN'T FINGERPRINTS. THERE'S *NOTHING*. NO DUST, NO DIRT, NO FIBERS.

BUT THERE IS *THIS*.

I DON'T SEE ANYTHING.
OH, COME ON. IT MUST BE AT LEAST HALF A MILLIMETER ACROSS.

WHAT IS THAT?
A CLUE TO THE IDENTITY OF WHOEVER WROTE THIS.
DROP!
LOOKS LIKE A PIECE OF SOIL OR ROCK FRAGMENT. IF I CAN FIGURE OUT WHERE IT'S FROM, THAT MIGHT BE A LEAD.

CAN YOU REALLY DETERMINE THAT FROM SOMETHING SO SMALL?
NOT EVERYONE CAN. BUT THEN...I'M NOT EVERYONE. YOU MADE THE RIGHT CALL, BRINGING THIS TO ME.

WAIT! THAT'S IT? YOU'RE GOING?
YES. I HAVE WORK TO DO.

BUT ACCORDING TO THE NOTE, SPYDER...OR WHOEVER SENT IT...IS COMING FOR ME SOON.

AND YOU WERE HOPING I'D PROTECT YOU?
WELL...YES. ARE THEY COMING TO KILL ME?
I DOUBT IT.
CAPTURE ME?

FAR MORE LIKELY.

OR PERHAPS THEY'RE JUST COMING TO HAVE A NICE TALK WITH ME.

DON'T GET YOUR HOPES UP. SPYDER OBVIOUSLY SEES SOME POTENTIAL IN YOU. I'M NOT SURE WHY, EXACTLY, BUT THEY DO.

ERICA...ARE YOU ANGRY AT ME?

YOU? NO. I'M NOT ANGRY AT *YOU*. DON'T WORRY ABOUT SPYDER, BEN. I'VE GOT YOUR BACK.

LATER...
RIP!

HEY, SMOKESCREEN. I WAS HOPING I'D SEE YOU BEFORE I LEFT. WE GOT OUR FIELD ASSIGNMENTS TODAY, SO YOU'RE GETTING IN JUST UNDER THE WIRE.

WHERE ARE YOU GOING?
VANCOUVER.
VANCOUVER? THAT'S NOT SO BAD.
OH, COME ON. IT'S IN *CANADA*.

I HEAR IT'S REALLY BEAUTIFUL. AND IT'S SUPPOSED TO HAVE GREAT RESTAURANTS...

YOU KNOW WHAT IT *DOESN'T* HAVE? CRIME. IT WAS RANKED THE SECOND SAFEST CITY IN THE WORLD LAST YEAR. ITS HOMICIDE RATE IS ALMOST NONEXISTENT. WHAT KIND OF FIELD EXPERIENCE AM I GONNA GET THERE?

ER...I HEAR THERE'S A LOT OF ILLEGAL WILDLIFE TRAFFICKING.

I DON'T WANT TO BUST SOME LAME PANDA SMUGGLERS! I WANT TO GO SOMEWHERE *DANGEROUS*. MOGADISHU. BOGOTÁ. ANYWHERE IN PAKISTAN. AND THEY'RE SENDING ME TO VANCOUVER. THIS IS THE WORST.

? ?

IS THAT A GOOD-BYE NOTE? AWWWW. YOU'RE SO SWEET...
UH, ACTUALLY... IT'S NOT A NOTE FOR *YOU*.

Hey, Ben!
Just wanted to let you know we'll be coming for you soon.
Your pals at SPYDER

YOU HAVE TO BE KIDDING! I'M BEING SHIPPED TO THE SAFEST PLACE ON THE PLANET WHILE YOU'RE GETTING SUCKED INTO MORE INTERNATIONAL INTRIGUE? IT'S NOT FAIR!

YOU'RE ONLY A FIRST YEAR AND YOU'RE ALREADY RECEIVING DEATH THREATS! DO YOU HAVE ANY IDEA HOW LUCKY YOU ARE?

I WAS ACTUALLY HOPING IT WAS MORE OF A CAPTURE THREAT...

I'LL NEVER GET A DEATH THREAT. CERTAINLY NOT IN VANCOUVER.

SHOVE!

DO YOU KNOW WHAT THE PROPER PROTOCOL FOR THIS IS?

I'D HELP, BUT I'M SHIPPING OUT TONIGHT. I'LL NEED TO PASS ON THE BATON TO YOUR RESIDENT ADVISER FOR NEXT YEAR.

WHO'S THAT?

HERE HE IS NOW. SPEAK OF THE DEVIL.

CHIP NEVER TOLD ME HE HAD A BROTHER.
THAT'S BECAUSE HE DOESN'T LIKE ME.
I'VE JUST SPENT A SEMESTER ABROAD, STUDYING IN LONDON AT THE TOP-SECRET SCHOOL FOR BRITISH AGENTS.

BEN'S JUST RECEIVED A DEATH THREAT. I'M HEADING OVER TO INFORM THE ADMINISTRATION.

SCRIBBLE SCRIBBLE!

TINA CUEV
VANCOU
1-60

IF YOU RUN INTO MORE TROUBLE, HERE'S MY NUMBER.

AND IN CASE I DON'T SEE YOU BEFORE I LEAVE...

...BE STRONG.

SPIN!

LET'S TAKE A WALK.

LET'S GET A COUPLE OF THINGS STRAIGHT HERE. NUMBER ONE: I DON'T LIKE YOU.
WHY NOT?

I UNDERSTAND YOU'RE FRIENDS WITH MY BROTHER.

YES.

I HATE MY BROTHER. THEREFORE, I HATE MY BROTHER'S FRIENDS. THEREFORE, I HATE YOU.
NUMBER TWO: YOU'RE TROUBLE. AND WHEN A STUDENT IS TROUBLE, HIS RESIDENTIAL ADVISER ENDS UP LOOKING BAD. LOOK WHAT HAPPENED TO TINA.

THAT'S NOT *MY* FAULT.
NO MATTER HOW YOU SLICE IT, YOU WERE INVOLVED.

I INTEND TO RUN A TIGHT SHIP HERE—AND I DON'T WANT ANY PROBLEMS FROM MY STUDENTS.
SHOVE!

THAT WOULD MAKE ME VERY ANGRY, UNDERSTAND?
NOD NOD!

GOOD. I'LL SEE YOU ON MONDAY.
YOU'LL BE AT SPY CAMP TOO?
OF COURSE. I'M NOT JUST YOUR RESIDENTIAL ADVISER. I'M ALSO YOUR CAMP COUNSELOR.

LUCKY ME.

THE NEXT DAY...
ARCADES
mini
Golf
Batting
Center

FUNLAND
AMUSEMENT CENTER
FUNLAND
REUSABLE
BEVERAGE
GOBLET
$20
BEN, THIS IS AGENT HAMILTON, PART OF YOUR CIA SECURITY DETAIL.

I FEEL LIKE THIS IS A MISTAKE COMING HERE.
I HAVE TO SEE MIKE. HE'S MY BEST FRIEND AND NOW, BECAUSE OF SPY CAMP, THIS IS THE ONLY TIME I'LL GET TO SEE HIM ALL SUMMER. I HAVEN'T EVEN BEEN ABLE TO TELL HIM ABOUT THAT YET.
BESIDES, SPYDER WON'T TRY TO DO ANYTHING AT A PLACE THIS PUBLIC, WILL THEY?

NOT IF WE CAN HELP IT.
SNACKO'S
FUNLAND MEMBERSHIP
DAILY EXP

WE'VE GOT THE ENTIRE PLACE COVERED.

LET'S HOPE HE TAKES THIS WELL.

DONK!
CRACK!

CRACK!

WHIZZ!

CAMP?!
WHAT ON EARTH DO YOU WANT TO GO THERE FOR? CAMP STINKS.

WOW!
CRACK!

THIS ONE'S SUPPOSED TO BE A LOT OF FUN.
SWING!
WHIZZ!

THAT'S WHAT THEY ALL SAY. AND THEN YOU GET THERE AND FIND OUT THEY THINK "FUN" MEANS GETTING MAULED BY MOSQUITOES AND POOPING IN AN OUTHOUSE.
IT'S BAD ENOUGH YOU HAD TO SWITCH SCHOOLS. NOW YOU'LL BE GONE ALL SUMMER, TOO?

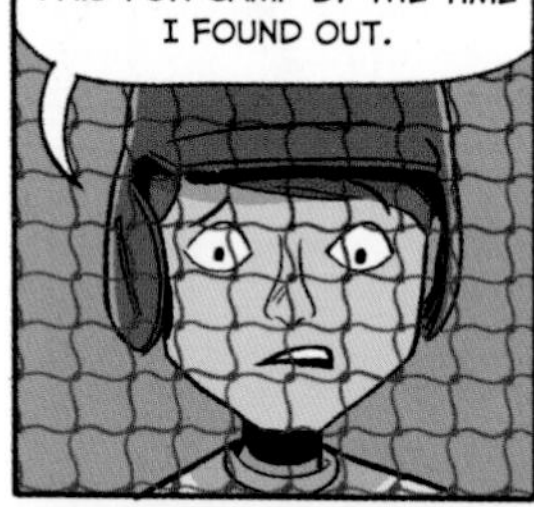
I'M SORRY. I *THOUGHT* I WAS GOING TO BE HERE TOO. MY PARENTS HAD ALREADY PAID FOR CAMP BY THE TIME I FOUND OUT.

WOW!
CLAP CLAP!
CRACK!
CHEER!

WHIZZ!

JEEZ, BEN. YOU'RE REALLY BAD AT THIS.
HEY! YOU'RE SUPPOSED TO BE PROTECTING ME. NOT MOCKING ME.

DONK!
HEE HEE HEE!

HA
HA
HA
HA
HA
HA
HA

HEY, BEN. HOW'S IT GOING?

WHIZZ!

MURRAY? WHAT ARE YOU DOING HERE? YOU'RE SUPPOSED TO BE UNDER MAXIMUM SECURITY AT...
...THE APPLE VALLEY REFORMATION CAMP FOR DELINQUENT TEENS? YEAH. I'M HERE ON BEHALF OF SPYDER. I THOUGHT WE COULD TALK...

LAST TIME WE TALKED, YOU TRIED TO KILL ME.

AND *YOU* KNOCKED ME UNCONSCIOUS!

TO PREVENT YOU FROM KILLING ME!

LET'S NOT GET ALL WRAPPED UP IN WHO DOUBLE-CROSSED WHO AND WHO TRIED TO FRAME THE OTHER ONE FOR TREASON...

THAT WAS ALL YOU!

IS THIS GUY BOTHERING YOU, BEN?
MAYBE NOW ISN'T THE BEST TIME TO TALK. WE'LL CATCH UP LATER.

mini Golf
TOSS!

BEN! WHERE ARE YOU GOING?
MURRAY HILL IS HERE! I'M IN PURSUIT!

STAND DOWN, RIPLEY!
WE'LL HANDLE THIS!

CRASH!
SLAM!

CRASH!
WHIZZ!
CRACK!
BALLS

VOLCANIC
PANIC!

SORRY!
I'LL GIVE IT BACK.

AAAAAHH!!!
SNAP!
OOOF!!
BOO
FLIP FLOP

WHOA!
ZZZT

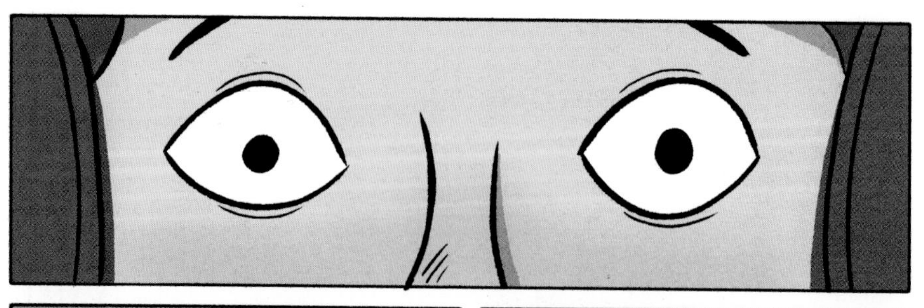

WE'LL BE IN
TOUCH, BEN!

SCREECH!

THIS IS WHY I TOLD YOU TO STAND DOWN.

IT WAS AN EMERGENCY!

IT WAS A WILD GOOSE CHASE. I ALREADY CALLED IT IN.

MURRAY HILL IS CURRENTLY STILL UNDER MAXIMUM SECURITY AT THE APPLE VALLEY REFORMATION CAMP FOR DELINQUENT TEENS.

THEN SOMETHING'S MESSED UP. I KNOW MURRAY HILL AND THAT WAS HIM.
MAYBE YOU CLOCKED YOURSELF HARDER THAN YOU REALIZED WITH ONE OF THOSE BASEBALLS.
MY HEAD'S WORKING PERFECTLY FINE. I EVEN GOT THE LICENSE PLATE: VGG-228. MAYBE YOU SHOULD SEE IF THAT'S A LEAD.
FINE. I'LL GO CALL IT IN.

NO POINT GETTING A JOB *HERE* THIS SUMMER. THIS PLACE IS TOAST.

MONDAY MORNING.
SCHOOL BUS

HAPPY TRAILS
WILDERNESS CAMP
OR BOYS AND GIRLS

HAPPY TRAILS
OFFICE
WELCOME!!

VELCOME

SMOKESCREEN! YOU MADE IT! YOUR BUS WAS THE LAST TO ARRIVE.
WE BETTER GET YOU TO YOUR CABIN BEFORE ALL THE GOOD BUNKS ARE TAKEN.

TOO LATE.
CHAMELEON!

WE'RE IN THE SAME CABIN?
THAT'S RIGHT! YOU'RE BOTH MUSKRATS!

MUSKRATS?

ALL THE BUNKHOUSES HAVE ANIMAL THEMES: MUSKRAT, BEAVER, OPOSSUM. I'M A POLLIWOG.
I WISH I COULD BE A MUSKRAT, BUT THERE'S NO COED LIVING AT HAPPY TRAILS.
THE BOYS' AND GIRLS' CABINS ARE ON SEPARATE SIDES OF CAMP.

THE ARMORY'S A LITTLE DIFFERENT THAN THE ONE AT SPY SCHOOL. IT'S MORE OF A FRONTIER FOCUS—THEY'VE GOT BOWS AND ARROWS AND TOMAHAWKS.
HAPPY TRAILS

SO WE CAN DEFEND OURSELVES IF WE EVER TIME TRAVEL BACK TO THE 1700S?

ARTS & CRAFTS
ARTS AND CRAFTS?
WITH AN ESPIONAGE ANGLE. TOMORROW, THEY'RE GONNA SHOW US HOW TO WHITTLE OUR OWN SPEARS.

WHO ARE THEY? NEW RECRUITS?

EXCHANGE STUDENTS. THEY'RE FROM THE MI6 ACADEMY IN ENGLAND.
THEY DON'T HAVE ANY FACILITIES LIKE HAPPY TRAILS OVER THERE, THOUGH, SO A TROOP OF THEM COMES HERE EVERY SUMMER.

CLAIRE HUTCHINS, THIS IS BEN RIPLEY, THE GUY I TOLD YOU ABOUT.

YOUR REPUTATION PRECEDES YOU. IT'S A PLEASURE.
THE PLEASURE'S ALL MINE.

HAPPY TRAILS
SMACK!

HAPPY TRAILS

THIS IS YOUR BIG-SHOT STUDENT?

HAPPY TRAILS

I WAS BEING FRIENDLY TOO. IF I'D WANTED TO BE MEAN, I'D HAVE RIPPED YOUR ARM FROM ITS SOCKET.

THAT WAS AMAZING, HOW YOU LET CLAIRE FLIP YOU OVER SO EASILY. TOTALLY TRICKED HER INTO THINKING YOU'RE A WUSS.
MAN, THE NEXT TIME SHE TRIES ANYTHING ON YOU, SHE'S GONNA BE SORRY.
BEN WASN'T FAKING. SHE REALLY DID FLIP HIM OVER.
HAPPY TRAILS

DON'T BE SUCH A DORK. SMOKESCREEN ONCE TOOK OUT AN ASSASSIN WITH JUST A TENNIS RACKET.
YOU THINK HE'S GONNA LET SOME CRUMPET SUCKER GET THE DROP ON HIM?

YOU TWO LOVEBIRDS WANT TO STOP BICKERING? I CAN BARELY HEAR MYSELF THINK.
I DIDN'T KNOW YOU *COULD* THINK.
HAPPY TRAILS
PAT PAT!

YOU'RE LUCKY YOU'RE A GIRL. IF WARREN HAD SAID THAT TO ME, YOU'D BE DIGGING HIM OUT OF THE LATRINE RIGHT NOW.

YOUR BROTHER'S MY CAMP COUNSELOR.

OH. SORRY ABOUT THAT.

WHY DIDN'T YOU EVER TELL ME ABOUT HIM?

'CAUSE HE'S A DORKWAD.

WHEN WE WERE KIDS, HIS FAVORITE HOBBY WAS SENDING ME TO THE EMERGENCY ROOM.
LET'S FIGURE OUT WHERE HIS BUNK IS AND PUT SOME FIRE ANTS IN IT.

MUSKRATS

WHAT'S THIS FOR?
TO KEEP WILDLIFE FROM GETTING IN AT NIGHT. AND ASSASSINS.

STINKS TO BE YOU. LOOKS LIKE YOU'RE SLEEPING UNDER NATE MACKEY.
IS HE STILL STRUGGLING WITH STRESS-INDUCED BED WETTING?
EVERY NIGHT.

WHERE'S YOUR BUNK?

OVER THERE.

SWITCH WITH BEN.

WHY SHOULD I DO THAT?

BECAUSE IF YOU DON'T, I'LL TEAR OUT YOUR KIDNEYS AND SMACK YOU SENSELESS WITH THEM.

YOU CAN HAVE MY BUNK. I DIDN'T LIKE THE VIEW ANYHOW.

WHAT'S THAT?
ADMINISTRATION.

YOU MEAN, FOR THE PRINCIPAL?

THE PRINCIPAL? HE WOULDN'T BE CAUGHT DEAD OUT HERE.
THE GUY'S TERRIFIED OF NATURE. WOODCHUCK RUNS THE CAMP.
HAPPY

WHO'S WOODCHUCK?

YOU'VE NEVER HEARD OF "WOODCHUCK" WALLACE?

NO.
RING!

Incoming Call
CODE RED.
URGENT.
ANSWER NOW.

COULD YOU GUYS EXCUSE ME?

BEN, THIS IS AGENT HAMILTON. I WAS WITH YOU AT FUNLAND AMUSEMENT PARK THE OTHER DAY.
SLAM!
OH! DID YOU TRACK DOWN MURRAY HILL YET?
NO. I'M HAVING SOME TROUBLE WITH THAT LICENSE PLATE NUMBER YOU GAVE US. ARE YOU SURE IT WAS CORRECT?

VIRGINIA VGG-228. I GUARANTEE THAT WAS IT. WHY?

I'M NOT AT LIBERTY TO DISCLOSE THAT TO YOU AT THIS TIME.
WHY NOT?
I'M NOT AT LIBERTY TO DISCLOSE THAT, EITHER.

I'M THE ONE WHO SPYDER IS TARGETING HERE! EXACTLY HOW MUCH MORE INVOLVED DO I NEED TO BE BEFORE SOMEONE CAN TELL ME WHAT'S GOING ON?
GIVE ME A FEW MINUTES. I'LL SEE WHAT I CAN DO.
ALL RIGHT.

YOU MUST BE AGENT WALLACE.
CALL ME WOODCHUCK.

ARRRR...
WAIT!

RRRAAAHH!!
SPLASH!

HEY! I NEEDED THAT!
NOBODY *NEEDS* A MOBILE PHONE. THEY'RE JUST SHACKLES TO CIVILIZATION.
ALL ANYONE REALLY NEEDS IN THIS WORLD IS THE BOUNTY THAT NATURE PROVIDES.

JERKY?

IT'S OPOSSUM. I MADE IT MYSELF.
CHOMP!

YOU DON'T UNDERSTAND.

OH, I DO. ONE DAY SOON, YOU'LL THANK ME FOR TOSSING AWAY THAT PHONE.
CHEW CHEW!

I WAS TALKING TO CIA HEADQUARTERS. I WAS GETTING AN UPDATE ON THE ENEMY GROUP THAT'S BEEN TARGETING ME.

AH. YOU MUST BE RIPLEY.

I ASSUME YOU'VE BEEN BRIEFED ON MY SITUATION?

YES. AND REST ASSURED, YOU'LL BE JUST AS SAFE HERE AS YOU WERE BACK IN SCHOOL.

I WASN'T REALLY THAT SAFE AT SCHOOL.

WELL, THIS FACILITY IS EXTREMELY WELL PROTECTED. PLUS, YOU'VE GOT *ME* LOOKING OUT FOR YOU.

SCHWANG!

NOT BAD.

LOOK CLOSER.

HOLY COW.
BUZZ BUZZ!

OF COURSE, IT ONLY DOES SO MUCH GOOD FOR *ME* TO LOOK AFTER YOU.
IT'S BETTER FOR YOU TO LEARN TO LOOK OUT FOR YOURSELF. THAT'S WHAT I'M GOING TO TEACH YOU THIS SUMMER. HOW TO SURVIVE ANYTHING:
PULL!
BOFF!
DROWNING,
LANDSLIDE,
BEAR ATTACKS...

HOW ABOUT BAD GUYS COMING AFTER ME WITH GUNS?

ONCE YOU'VE GONE A WEEK IN THE WILDERNESS SURVIVING ON NOTHING BUT YOUR WITS AND PEAT MOSS, BAD GUYS WITH GUNS WILL BE A PIECE OF CAKE.
TOSS!
IS THE PEAT MOSS THING A PART OF THE STANDARD MENU OUT HERE?

NOPE. BUT I'VE BEEN GIVEN SPECIAL ORDERS TO WHIP YOU INTO SHAPE.
LUCKY ME.
SETTLE IN AND GET UNPACKED. YOUR TRAINING STARTS FIRST THING TOMORROW.

LEAP!
SPIN!

WOW. WOODCHUCK WALLACE IS GOING TO PERSONALLY OVERSEE YOUR SURVIVAL TRAINING! YOU'RE GOING TO END UP AN EVEN MORE AWESOME SPY THAN YOU ALREADY ARE!
WHY DO *YOU* GET SUCH SPECIAL TREATMENT?
HAPPY TRAILS

IT'S NOT EXACTLY A REWARD. YOU GUYS ARE GONNA BE SITTING AROUND A CAMPFIRE MAKING S'MORES, AND I'LL BE IN A CAVE EATING RAW GRASSHOPPERS.

YOU DON'T GET TO MAKE ANY S'MORES AS A SPY. THIS *IS* A REWARD.
SO HOW ABOUT ANSWERING THE QUESTION THIS TIME: WHY WOULD HE FOCUS ON *YOU*?

I'VE GOT AN EVEN BETTER QUESTION, RIPLEY. WHAT'S ALL THIS ABOUT?
HAPPY TRAILS

WHERE'D YOU GET THAT?

MY FOOTLOCKER. THE FOOTLOCKER THAT WAS SUPPOSED TO BE *YOURS.*

IT WAS IN THIS.

BEN RIPLEY: CLASSIFIED
BEN RIPLEY:
BEN RIPLEY: CLASSIFIED
BEN RIPLEY
N RIPLEY: CLASSIFIED
BEN RIPLEY: CLASSIFIED

YOU OPENED MY CLASSIFIED MAIL?
IT SEEMED SUSPICIOUS. AND MY INSTINCTS WERE RIGHT. IT'S FROM MURRAY HILL.

GRAB!

Hey, Ben!

Sorry we didn't get a chance to talk the other day. I was hoping to give you a heads-up about this. I know all the legalese can give you a headache just to look at, so here's the gist:

SPYDER is working on a very big project that requires the services of someone with your special skills. We could really use your help on this one, and we're prepared to pay you well for it.

That said, while we want you to work with us, we really don't want you to work against us. So either you join us—or we'll kill you. That's not an idle threat. As you've no doubt figured out, we can get into spy camp easily.

If you're in, sign this contract and leave it in the hollow tree stump by the entry gate, and we'll extract you. If you're out, well...it was nice knowing you. You have twenty-four hours to decide.

Murray

Contents

1. WARRANTIES
2. CONFIDENTIALITY AGREEMENT
3. INSURANCE
4. VACATION TIME
5. PENSION
6. COMPENSATION PACKAGE
7. FORCE MAJEURE
8. TERMINATION CLAUSE

8. TERMINATION CLAUSE

If the party of the first part (Ripley) opts not to engage in business with the party of the second part (SPYDER), then SPYDER reserves the right to terminate the existence of Ripley in the manner in which they see fit.

In the event that Ripley is determined to merely be pretending to provide services for SPYDER while, in actuality, continuing to act in the capacity of a federal agent, then SPYDER shall retaliate in a manner such as, but not limited to, the following: the removal of Ripley's head by force from the rest of his body, extraction of Ripley's cerebellum via his nasal passages, excessive bludgeoning, or defenestration.

MINUTES LATER...

WHOA. THIS IS SERIOUS.

I KNOW. WHAT SHOULD WE DO ABOUT IT?
FIRST OF ALL, WE BEEF UP SECURITY AROUND THE CAMP. ESPECIALLY AROUND YOUR CABIN.
I'LL SET UP A FEW EXTRA SNARES AND TIGER TRAPS AND SUCH TO KEEP OUT ANYONE FROM SPYDER.
BUT BEYOND THAT, WELL...I HAVE TO ADMIT, THIS IS A BIT OUT OF MY LEAGUE.

BUT YOU'RE IN CHARGE HERE.

I TEACH SURVIVAL SKILLS. NOT COUNTER-TERRORISM. I'LL HAVE TO REPORT THIS TO MY SUPERIORS.
GRAB SOME GRUB. I SHOULD HAVE A RESPONSE FROM THE CIA BY THE TIME YOU'RE DONE.

I SHOULDN'T HAVE TO TELL YOU, BUT SPYDER'S EXISTENCE IS HIGHLY CLASSIFIED.
NO ONE ELSE IS TO KNOW. BEN SHOULDN'T HAVE EVEN SHARED THIS INFORMATION WITH THE THREE OF YOU.
HAPPY TRAILS

I DIDN'T. THIS WAS SPYDER'S DOING. THEY LEFT THE CONTRACT IN THE WRONG FOOTLOCKER.
NOD NOD
WHATEVER THE CASE, KEEP IT QUIET.
NOD NOD
RUSTLE RUSTLE
HAPPY TRAILS

MESS HALL.

I'VE BEEN THINKING...BEN SAID SPYDER PUT THE CONTRACT IN THE WRONG FOOTLOCKER, BUT THEY DIDN'T–
WE'RE NOT SUPPOSED TO BE TALKING ABOUT SPYDER!
HAPPY TRAILS

OKAY, HOW ABOUT WE CALL IT...

HAPPY TRAILS

...SPORK?

ANYHOW, SPORK DIDN'T GET THE WRONG LOCKER. THEY GOT THE RIGHT ONE; THEY JUST DIDN'T PREDICT THAT YOU GUYS WOULD SWITCH BUNKS.
WHICH MEANS THAT WHOEVER DELIVERED THAT CONTRACT FOR SPORK MUST HAVE BEEN KEEPING A CLOSE EYE ON MUSKRAT CABIN.
MAYBE SPORK'S MAN IS INSIDE MUSKRAT CABIN.

HEY, YOU'RE IN MUSKRAT CABIN. WE NEVER ACTUALLY SAW YOU TAKE THE CONTRACT OUT OF THE FOOTLOCKER. MAYBE YOU JUST SAID YOU FOUND IT.

I DID FIND IT! I SWEAR!

RELAX, I'M JUST JERKING YOUR CHAIN. AS IF SPORK WOULD EVER HIRE A WHACK-JOB LIKE YOU.
HA HA, VERY FUNNY. AN ENEMY ORGANIZATION HAS INFILTRATED OUR SCHOOL, SMOKESCREEN'S LIFE IS UNDER THREAT, AND IT'S ALL JUST ONE BIG JOKE TO YOU.

IT'S NOTHING. WE WERE JUST IMAGINING HYPOTHETICAL DANGEROUS SCENARIOS SO WE'D BE PREPARED IF THEY OCCURRED.

WHAT KIND OF SCENARIO WERE YOU IMAGINING?

HAPPY TRAILS

WHY NOT LET BRAINIAC AND POTATOHEAD PLAY TOO? AT LEAST BRAINIAC MIGHT HAVE SOME IDEAS ON THE SUBJECT.
WHICH ONE OF US IS BRAINIAC?
HAPPY TRAILS

I'LL GIVE YOU A HINT. IT'S NOT YOU.

OKAY, LET'S HEAR IT.

WHAT IF ONE OF US WERE BEING TARGETED BY AN ENEMY ORGANIZATION? THEY WANT YOU TO DO SOMETHING FOR THEM WITHIN TWENTY-FOUR HOURS. AND IF YOU DON'T, THEY'LL KILL YOU.

YOU COULD ALWAYS JUST DO WHAT THE BAD GUYS ASKED.
YES, IF YOU'RE A WUSS. FOR THE SAKE OF TIME, LET'S SAY THE TARGET IS SMOKESCREEN.

WELL, IF IT'S YOU, THAT'S EASY. FIRST THING YOU DO IS...

GO ASK ERICA FOR HELP.

THAT'S RIGHT. THAT'S EXACTLY WHAT YOU SHOULD DO!
SHE LIKES YOU MORE THAN ANYONE ELSE HERE. SHE ACTUALLY PUT HER ARM AROUND YOU ONCE.

SHE PUT HER ARM AROUND ME ONCE, TOO.
THAT WAS IN MARTIAL ARTS CLASS AND SHE WAS FLIPPING YOU ONTO YOUR BACK. IT'S NOT THE SAME THING.

ZOE'S RIGHT. YOU SHOULD GO TO ERICA. PROTECT YOURSELF ANY WAY YOU CAN. MY LIFE HASN'T BEEN THREATENED, AND *I'M* TOTALLY ON EDGE.

WHAT'S GOING ON HERE?
I MEAN, I'M ON EDGE *IN THEORY.*

BANG!

MY, MY. YOU YANKS CERTAINLY ARE A TWITCHY LOT.
THAT WASN'T FUNNY!

NOT TO YOU, PERHAPS. BUT TO EVERYONE ELSE, IT WAS.

LET'S SEE HOW FUNNY YOU THINK IT IS WHEN I PUNCH YOUR FACE IN.

STAND DOWN, ZOE! I DON'T WANT ANY SHENANIGANS!
HAPPY TRAILS

SHE STARTED IT!

I SAID STAND DOWN!

WE DON'T REALLY KNOW THOSE GUYS AT ALL, DO WE? MAYBE ONE OF THEM IS THE DOUBLE AGENT.

I SUPPOSE THAT'S POSSIBLE.

OH MY GOSH! IT'S ALEXANDER HALE!

BENJAMIN! JUST THE MAN I'M HERE TO SEE.
THANK GOODNESS YOU'RE ALL RIGHT.

I HEAR YOU'VE RECEIVED A DEATH THREAT FROM OUR OLD FRIENDS AT YOU-KNOW-WHERE.

IT WAS MORE LIKE A CONTRACT FOR A JOB.
REALLY? WELL, IN THE WRONG HANDS, EVEN PAPER CAN BE DEADLY.

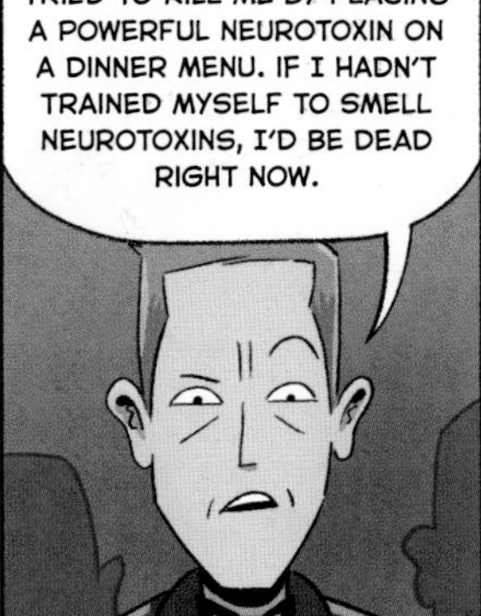
ONCE, WHEN I WAS IN BANGLADESH, MY ENEMIES TRIED TO KILL ME BY PLACING A POWERFUL NEUROTOXIN ON A DINNER MENU. IF I HADN'T TRAINED MYSELF TO SMELL NEUROTOXINS, I'D BE DEAD RIGHT NOW.

MAYBE WE SHOULD DISCUSS THIS SOMEWHERE MORE PRIVATE.

I WAS JUST ABOUT TO SUGGEST THAT MYSELF. GOOD TO SEE YOU'RE AS NIMBLE OF MIND AS I.

COULD YOU ALL MAKE YOURSELVES SCARCE FOR A FEW MINUTES? AGENT RIPLEY AND I HAVE SOMETHING OF GREAT IMPORTANCE TO DISCUSS.

I'M JUST CHECKING FOR BUGS–YOU KNOW, LISTENING DEVICES.

STOMP!
AND COCKROACHES.

WHAT'S GOING ON?
I'M HERE ON DIRECT ORDERS FROM THE HIGHEST LEVEL. I WAS TOLD TO COME ASAP. THUS, MY RATHER UNORTHODOX ATTIRE.
WHAT ARE YOU SUPPOSED TO DO?

I'VE BEEN ASSIGNED AS LEAD AGENT ON THIS INVESTIGATION. I'M QUITE THE MASTER OF CAMOUFLAGE, AS YOU KNOW. I ONCE SPENT THREE DAYS IN A TERRORIST DEN DISGUISED AS A ROCK.

SURE YOU DID.

YOU WON'T EVEN KNOW I'M HERE. AND MOST IMPORTANT, NEITHER WILL SPYDER.

IF SPYDER'S KEEPING AN EYE ON THE CAMP, THEN THEY ALREADY KNOW YOU'RE HERE. YOU COULDN'T HAVE PICKED A FLASHIER WAY OF SHOWING UP THAN PARACHUTING DOWN IN A TUXEDO.

INTIMIDATION, MY YOUNG FRIEND. I *WANTED* THEM TO SEE ME. NOW THEY KNOW IF THEY WANT TO GET TO YOU, THEY HAVE TO GO THROUGH ME.
THAT'LL MAKE THEM THINK TWICE ABOUT COMING AFTER YOU. NOW THAT I'M HERE, YOU CAN REST EASY.

MUSKRATS DORMITORY 5:00 A.M.
ZZZZZZ
ZZZZ
ZZZZ
ZZZZZ
ZZZZ
ZZ
ZZZ
ZZZZ
CRASH!
GET UP, MUSKRATS! NOW, NOW, NOW!
CLANG!
CLANG!

SPRING!

BOING!

SPLAT!

MOVE IT, YOU MAGGOTS! THIS ISN'T A RESORT— THIS IS A TRAINING FACILITY!
LAST ONE OUT THE DOOR DOES AN EXTRA FIFTY PUSH-UPS!

I WANT FIFTY PUSH-UPS OUT OF YOU.
BUT I'M NOT THE LAST ONE OUT.
NO ONE EVER SAID LIFE WAS FAIR.

36...
37...
38...

WHY ARE *YOU* DOING PUSH-UPS?
A LITTLE EXTRA UPPER-BODY STRENGTH NEVER HURT ANYONE.

FIFTY PUSH-UPS!
EVERYONE ELSE DOES JUMPING JACKS UNTIL HE FINISHES THEM ALL!
GROAN

WHOEVER DID THAT JUST BOUGHT ALL OF YOU AN EXTRA MILE THIS MORNING.
WE'LL START WITH THE CHALLENGE TRAIL AROUND THE WOODS, FOLLOWED BY DEADMAN'S ROUTE UP MOUNT ROOSEVELT.

MOVE OUT!

SNAP!
WHOA!
SLAM!
YANK!

Y'KNOW, WHEN MOST PEOPLE WANT TO TALK TO SOMEONE ELSE, THEY CALL THEM ON THE PHONE. OR MAYBE DROP BY THEIR ROOM. THEY DON'T AMBUSH THEM IN THE MIDDLE OF THE WOODS.

IT'S IN BOTH OF OUR BEST INTERESTS IF NO ONE KNOWS WE'RE ALIGNED ON THIS MATTER.

WHERE ARE WE GOING?
TAKING A SHORTCUT BACK TO CAMP. UNLESS YOU WERE ENJOYING THE SCENIC ROUTE.

AS LONG AS HANK DOESN'T NOTICE I'M GONE. DO YOU BELIEVE I SAW MURRAY THE OTHER DAY?

WHY WOULDN'T I?

BECAUSE THE CIA DOESN'T. THE AGENT I TALKED TO CLAIMS HE'S LOCKED UP AT SOME JUVENILE REHABILITATION FACILITY.

YES, THAT STRUCK ME AS A BIT ODD AS WELL.
HOW CAN MURRAY BE IN TWO PLACES AT ONCE?
I'M STILL WORKING ON THAT. BUT I DID FIND OUT WHY EVERYONE WAS SO FREAKED OUT ABOUT THE LICENSE PLATE NUMBER YOU GOT.

YOU KNOW ABOUT THAT?

I'M TRAINING TO BE A SPY, BEN. IT'S MY JOB TO KNOW THINGS. THAT LICENSE PLATE BELONGS TO THE DIRECTOR OF THE CIA.

THE DIRECTOR OF THE CIA IS WORKING WITH SPYDER?

OH. SPYDER STOLE IT FROM HIM.
THE THING IS, THE DIRECTOR'S IDENTITY IS CLASSIFIED.

NO IT'S NOT. HE'S ON TV ALL THE TIME...

THAT'S JUST A DECOY. I MEAN THE *REAL* DIRECTOR OF THE CIA.
YOU MEAN THE GUY EVERYONE THINKS IS THE REAL LEADER IS A FAKE?

CORRECT. ALMOST NO ONE KNOWS WHO THE REAL LEADER IS. EVEN MOST CIA AGENTS. BUT SOMEHOW, SPYDER DOES.

WHY WOULD THEY
REVEAL THAT TO US?

TO SEND A MESSAGE: THEY KNOW *EVERYTHING.* AND THEY CAN GET TO ANYONE, ANYWHERE. SPYDER'S KEPT IN THE SHADOWS FOR YEARS.
ANY TIME THEY MAKE A PUBLIC APPEARANCE, IT'S A RISK. AND YET, SPYDER MUST THINK YOU'RE WORTH IT.

BUT WHY ME? IF THEY WANTED THE BEST AGENT AT SPY SCHOOL, WHY AREN'T THEY GOING AFTER YOU?

MAYBE YOU HAVE SOME LATENT TALENT THAT'S EXTREMELY IMPORTANT TO THEM.
A TALENT THAT EVEN I DON'T KNOW ABOUT? I HAVE NO IDEA WHAT SPYDER THINKS I CAN DO FOR THEM.

THEN LET'S FOCUS ON PROTECTING YOU. WHAT'S THE BEST WAY TO DO THAT?

GET TO THEM BEFORE THEY GET TO ME?
EXACTLY. AND HOW DO WE DO THAT?
WELL, THE EASIEST WAY FOR THEM TO BE DELIVERING THINGS LIKE THE NOTE AND CONTRACT TO ME WOULD BE TO HAVE ANOTHER MOLE ON THE INSIDE, RIGHT?
YES. IF NOT MORE THAN ONE MOLE.

SO IF WE CAN FIGURE OUT WHO IT IS, WE'RE ON THE RIGHT PATH.
ANY IDEA WHO IT MIGHT BE?
I WAS GOING TO ASK *YOU* THAT.

WHOEVER PUT THE CONTRACT IN THE FOOTLOCKER DID IT *AFTER* ALL OF THE BUNKS WERE CLAIMED— BUT BEFORE I ARRIVED. I SAW CLAIRE HUTCHINS AND THE REST OF HER MI6 GANG COMING FROM THE DIRECTION OF MY CABIN RIGHT BEFORE I GOT THERE.
INTERESTING. DID YOU SEE ANYONE ELSE NEAR YOUR CABIN?

NO. WELL, NO ONE EXCEPT ZOE, WARREN, AND CHIP.

ALSO INTERESTING.

THERE'S NO WAY ZOE'S THE MOLE. SHE'S MY FRIEND...

SO WAS MURRAY. AND LOOK HOW THAT TURNED OUT.

I DIDN'T REALLY KNOW MURRAY ALL THAT LONG. I'VE KNOWN ZOE FOR FIVE MONTHS.
YOU CAN'T TRUST ANYBODY.
I TRUST ZOE.

HOW ABOUT WARREN?
I DON'T THINK WARREN'S EXACTLY SPYDER MATERIAL.
NO ONE WOULD HAVE THOUGHT THAT ABOUT MURRAY, EITHER. IT TAKES AN AWFULLY GOOD DOUBLE AGENT TO CONVINCE YOU THAT THEY'RE A REALLY BAD REAL AGENT.
WARREN COULD HAVE DELIVERED THE CONTRACT. CHIP COULD HAVE TOO.

HOW ARE WE SUPPOSED TO GET DOWN?

?

YOU HAVE TO BE KIDDING.
HAVE YOU EVER KNOWN ME TO KID? STOP BEING SUCH A WEENIE AND GET ON THE WIRE.

HOW DID YOU EVEN KNOW ABOUT THIS?
IT'S MY–
"IT'S MY JOB TO KNOW THINGS"? YEAH, YEAH. BUT THIS PLACE IS HUGE. SOMEONE MUST HAVE SHOWN YOU AROUND. YOUR FATHER, MAYBE?

JOSHUA HALLAL?
NO. NOT MY FATHER.

LEAP!

I'M SORRY ABOUT JOSHUA.
WHY? IT'S NOT LIKE *YOU* KILLED HIM.
I MEANT, I SHOULDN'T HAVE BROUGHT IT UP. I KNOW JOSHUA WAS IMPORTANT TO YOU.
AND IT MEANS A LOT THAT YOU'RE HELPING ME AGAINST SPYDER, GIVEN WHAT THEY DID TO HIM.
I'M NOT ABOUT TO LET SPYDER KILL ANY MORE OF OUR AGENTS. AND I'M GOING TO MAKE THEM PAY FOR WHAT THEY DID TO JOSHUA.
TUCK IN YOUR LEGS. WE'RE COMING IN FOR A LANDING.
WHIZZ!
PULL!

BOING!

WE'LL HAVE TO MOVE QUICKLY SO HANK DOESN'T NOTICE YOU'RE GONE.

DID YOU EVER FIND OUT WHAT THAT SPECK ON THE FIRST NOTE FROM SPYDER WAS?
YES. IT WAS A FRAGMENT OF BITUMINOUS COAL.
THAT'S IT?

WHAT WERE YOU HOPING FOR? A CANISTER OF MICROFILM THAT DETAILED ALL OF SPYDER'S PLANS?

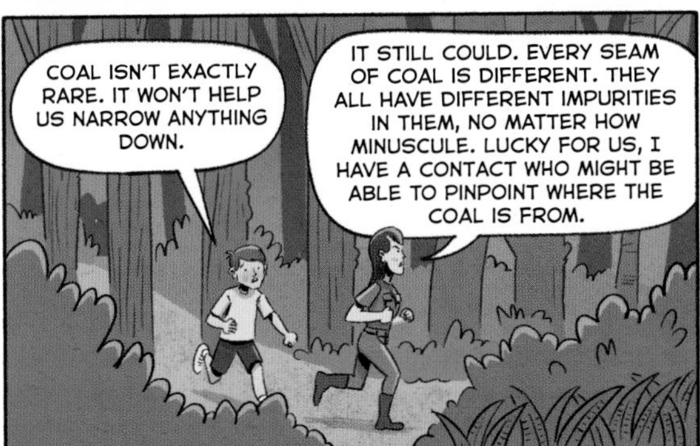
COAL ISN'T EXACTLY RARE. IT WON'T HELP US NARROW ANYTHING DOWN.
IT STILL COULD. EVERY SEAM OF COAL IS DIFFERENT. THEY ALL HAVE DIFFERENT IMPURITIES IN THEM, NO MATTER HOW MINUSCULE. LUCKY FOR US, I HAVE A CONTACT WHO MIGHT BE ABLE TO PINPOINT WHERE THE COAL IS FROM.

WHO?

SHHH!
PULL!
LOOKS LIKE YOUR SPOT.
SHOVE!

10 MINUTES LATER...

PANT
PANT!

YOU'RE RIGHT. I ONLY RAN THE FIRST MILE, MAGICALLY FOUND A SHORTCUT FROM A WILDERNESS AREA I'D NEVER SEEN BEFORE, AND THEN JUMPED BACK ONTO THE TRAIL WITH ONLY A FEW MINUTES TO GO.
MAYBE WE SHOULD RUN *TEN MILES* THIS AFTERNOON AND SEE HOW REFRESHED YOU FEEL THEN.

I'M AFRAID THERE WON'T BE TIME FOR ANOTHER RUN TODAY, BECAUSE YOUNG RIPLEY HERE IS LEAVING CAMP RIGHT AFTER BREAKFAST.
THAT'S AN ORDER STRAIGHT FROM THE TOP.

YOU LOSERS ARE IN TERRIBLE SHAPE! YOU'RE PATHETIC!

WHERE AM I GOING?
FAR FROM HERE. AND INTO SOME *SERIOUS* WILDERNESS.

THIS ISN'T SERIOUS WILDERNESS?
THIS PLACE IS A SPA COMPARED TO THE REAL THING. BUT REST ASSURED, THERE'S NOWHERE SAFER. SPYDER WILL NEVER BE ABLE TO FIND YOU OUT THERE. NOT WITH ME BY YOUR SIDE.

WHAT IF SPYDER IS ONTO US, THOUGH? COULDN'T THEY FOLLOW US INTO THE WILDERNESS?
YES. BUT WE HAVE A PLAN. WE'RE SENDING YOU OFF WITH A BUSLOAD OF YOUR FELLOW CAMPERS. YOU AND I WILL COVERTLY SLIP OFF THE BUS WHILE THE REST WILL CONTINUE ON AS DECOYS. SPYDER WON'T HAVE ANY IDEA WHERE WE'VE GONE.
YOU'RE SURE THAT WILL WORK?

OF COURSE IT WILL.
AND WHAT DOES ALEXANDER HALE THINK OF IT?

DOESN'T MATTER. I'VE BEEN PUT IN CHARGE OF YOUR SAFETY NOW. GET YOURSELF A GOOD BREAKFAST. WE'RE ONLY GOING TO EAT WHAT WE CAN FORAGE FOR THE NEXT FEW DAYS.

AFTER BREAKFAST...

SCHOOL BUS

SO YOU'RE GOING TOTAL SURVIVALIST OUT THERE?
APPARENTLY SO. THE AGENCY IS TRYING TO FIGURE OUT WHAT SPYDER IS UP TO.

BUT THE TWENTY-FOUR HOURS SPYDER GAVE ME ARE JUST ABOUT UP.
SO INSTEAD OF FORCING ME TO CHOOSE BETWEEN WORKING FOR THE ENEMY AND DEATH, THE CIA IS REMOVING ME FROM THE EQUATION.

YIKES. I HOPE OUR DRIVER KNOWS WHAT HE'S DOING.
IF HE MAKES ONE WRONG MOVE, WE'RE *ALL* GONNA BE DOING SURVIVAL TRAINING OUT HERE.

POP QUIZ: SUPPOSE THIS BUS FALLS INTO THE RAVINE, FORCING EVERYONE TO HAVE TO SURVIVE OUT HERE. WHAT'S THE FIRST THING YOU SHOULD DO?
EAT THE PEOPLE WHO DIDN'T MAKE IT?

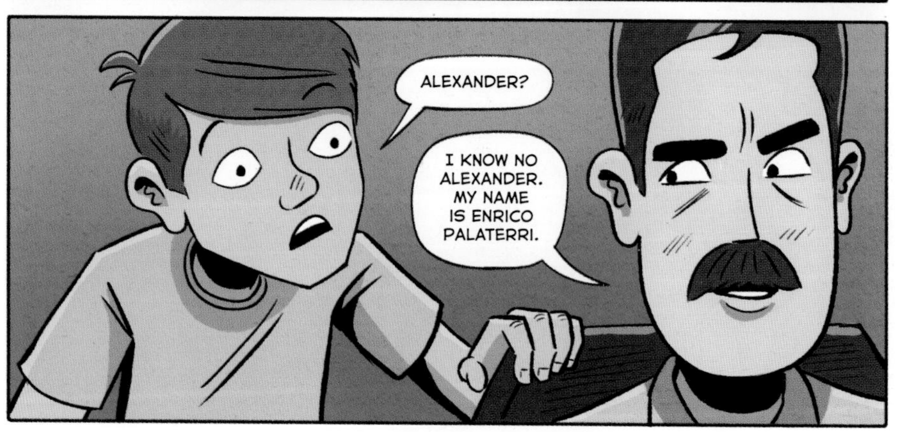
ALEXANDER?
I KNOW NO ALEXANDER. MY NAME IS ENRICO PALATERRI.

WHAT ARE YOU DOING HERE?
GETTING YOU TO YOUR DESTINATION SAFELY.

SCHOOL BUS

BUT YOU'RE NOT SUPPOSED TO BE PROTECTING ME ANYMORE. WOODCHUCK'S BEEN ASSIGNED TO DO THAT. YOU SHOULD BE FIGURING OUT WHAT SPYDER IS UP TO AND NEUTRALIZING THEM.
I DON'T KNOW WHAT YOU'RE TALKING ABOUT. I'M ONLY HERE TO DRIVE THE BUS.

I MADE AN EXECUTIVE DECISION. WOODCHUCK MIGHT BE A GREAT SURVIVALIST, BUT HE'S NOT A GREAT SPY. IF SPYDER COMES AFTER YOU, YOU'RE GOING TO NEED SOMEONE WITH MY SKILLS TO PROTECT YOU.

THE WHOLE IDEA WAS FOR YOU TO STOP THEM *BEFORE* THEY CAME AFTER ME.
BENJAMIN, RELAX. YOU'RE IN GOOD HANDS HERE. SPYDER ISN'T GOING TO BE ANY TROUBLE AT ALL.

AAAAH!!!
WE'RE GOING TO DIE!
BO

SCHOOL BUS
OM!

BOOM!
BENJAMIN RIPLEY, YOUR TWENTY-FOUR HOURS IS OFFICIALLY UP. KINDLY SURRENDER YOURSELF—OR WE WILL BLOW YOU AND EVERYONE ELSE TO SMITHEREENS.

OKAY! HOLD YOUR FIRE! I'M COMING OUT!
THEY'RE JUST BLUFFING.

BUS
SURE DOESN'T *LOOK* LIKE THEY'RE BLUFFING.

WE WARNED YOU NOT TO RUN, BENJAMIN!
SKIP!
CRUMBLE

YOU LEAVE US NO CHOICE!

HOOL BUS 100
I'M NOT RUNNING! I'M BEING DRAGGED AGAINST MY WILL! DON'T SHOOT! WHATEVER YOU WANT ME TO DO, I'LL DO!

LOCKED AND LOADED.
FIRE ON THREE.
ONE...

TWO...

WHIZZ!
CRACK!
AHHH!

CLATTER!

CLATTER!
DONK!

SWING!
SCHOOL BUS

SCHOOL BUS
BUS
WOOSH!
THUMP!

WHAT ON EARTH DO YOU THINK YOU'RE DOING?

WHAT *YOU'RE* SUPPOSED TO BE DOING. TAKING DOWN SPYDER.

BANG!
UH-OH.

BOOM!

DO SOMETHING USEFUL FOR ONCE.
COVER OUR ESCAPE.
SHOVE!
ERICA! WAIT...
WHAT PART OF "COVER OUR ESCAPE" DID YOU NOT UNDERSTAND?
YOU ALREADY CHASED OFF THE ENEMY.
YOU THINK SPYDER SENT ONLY TWO AGENTS TO DO THIS JOB?
GRAB!
BANG!
BANG!
BANG!
BANG!
PFUT
PFUT

DAD! SHOOT THEM!
I WOULD, BUT... I DON'T KNOW HOW TO WORK A GRENADE LAUNCHER.
WHAT?! I THOUGHT GRANDPA TAUGHT YOU.
HE *TRIED*. I JUST DIDN'T PAY ATTENTION.
IS THERE *ANYTHING* YOU CAN'T SCREW UP?
BANG!
BANG!
PFUT
PFUT
BANG!
WATCH YOUR TONE WITH ME, YOUNG WOMAN. I WAS DOING A PERFECTLY GOOD JOB HERE BEFORE YOU CAME ALONG.
BY LEADING THE PERSON YOU'RE PROTECTING OUT ONTO AN OPEN ROAD IN DIRECT LINE OF ENEMY FIRE?
ER...WELL...UH... WHAT EXACTLY WOULD *YOU* HAVE DONE IN THAT SITUATION?
IF I'D BEEN IN CHARGE, I WOULDN'T HAVE ALLOWED US TO GET *INTO* THAT SITUATION.

AND WHAT'S YOUR PLAN HERE? THERE'S EVEN LESS COVER OUT ON THE BRIDGE THAN ON THE ROAD.
BANG!
WE'RE NOT STAYING ON THE BRIDGE FOR LONG.
BANG!
BANG!
OH NO. TELL ME WE'RE NOT JUMPING.
OKAY. WE'RE NOT JUMPING.
BANG!
AAAAAHHHHHHH!!!!!
BANG!

POINT YOUR TOES AND KEEP YOUR ARMS TO YOUR SIDES, SO THAT THE IMPACT DOESN'T BREAK THEM.
SPLASH!

SLAP!

WE NEARLY DIED TEN TIMES.

BUT WE DIDN'T. SO WE'VE GOT THAT GOING FOR US.

BEFORE I SAVE YOU, I NEED YOU TO PROMISE ME SOMETHING.

NOW? I'M IN SERIOUS DANGER HERE.

SEEMS LIKE THE BEST TIME TO GET YOUR ATTENTION. PROMISE THAT, FROM HERE ON OUT, I'M IN CHARGE OF THIS OPERATION. I MAKE THE DECISIONS. YOU FOLLOW MY ORDERS, NO QUESTIONS ASKED.

SURE. WHATEVER YOU WANT. JUST HELP ME!

I ASKED YOU TO PROMISE.

ALL RIGHT! I PROMISE! YOU'RE IN CHARGE OF THIS OPERATION!
SWOOSH!

I THOUGHT I RAISED YOU BETTER THAN THAT.
YOU DIDN'T RAISE ME AT ALL. MOM DID.

COME ALONG, BENJAMIN. LET'S FIND OUR WAY TO SAFETY.
HAVE YOU ALREADY FORGOTTEN? YOU'RE NOT GIVING THE ORDERS HERE. YOU PROMISED I WAS IN CHARGE.
THAT AGREEMENT WAS LEGALLY NONBINDING! IT WAS MADE UNDER DURESS.

WE'RE NOT LISTENING TO YOU.
ERICA! I AM YOUR FATHER! YOU ARE JUST A GIRL! I KNOW YOU'VE HAD SOME MINOR SUCCESS IN THE SPY GAME–

SUCCESS THAT *YOU* TOOK THE CREDIT FOR!

–BUT YOU ARE NOT A FULL-FLEDGED AGENT YET. YOU ARE WAY OUT OF YOUR LEAGUE HERE.

I'M WAY OUT OF MY LEAGUE HERE? I'M ONLY IN THIS SITUATION BECAUSE YOU MESSED EVERYTHING UP!
BEN WOULD HAVE BEEN CAPTURED BY SPYDER IF IT WASN'T FOR ME.
THAT IS PATENTLY UNTRUE. I WAS LEADING US TO SAFETY WHEN YOU JUMPED OFF THAT BRIDGE LIKE A MANIAC.

SPYDER HAD AN AMBUSH WAITING FOR US ON THE OTHER SIDE OF THE BRIDGE.

GULP!

I KNEW THAT.
NO, YOU DIDN'T.
THUMP!

WHAT YOU DON'T KNOW COULD FILL A LIBRARY.

C'MON, BEN.

ET TU, BENJAMIN? ET TU?
YOU *DID* TAKE ALL THE CREDIT FOR CAPTURING MURRAY HILL.

THAT WAS FOR YOUR OWN GOOD! I DIDN'T WANT SPYDER TO KNOW OF YOUR ROLE IN THAT FOR FEAR THAT THEY'D RETALIATE.
SPYDER KNOWS EVERYTHING ABOUT EVERYTHING. THAT'S WHY WE'RE HERE RIGHT NOW.
THE ONLY PEOPLE YOU REALLY SNOWED WERE THE TOP BRASS AT THE CIA.

OH DEAR.

I THINK I HAVE A LEECH IN MY UNDERPANTS.

WHERE WERE YOU ON THE BUS?
I WAS STOWED AWAY IN THE BACK, WITH ALL THE SURVIVAL GEAR.
DID YOU KNOW SPYDER WAS GOING TO ATTACK US?

NO, BUT I HAD A HUNCH THEY MIGHT. THE BRILLIANT MINDS AT SPY SCHOOL PLAYED RIGHT INTO SPYDER'S HANDS.
AND NOW, THANKS TO MY FATHER, WE'RE MILES FROM CIVILIZATION, SOAKING WET, AND ALL OF OUR WEAPONS AND PHONES HAVE BEEN SWEPT DOWNRIVER.
BUT YOU HAVE A PLAN, RIGHT? YOU ALWAYS HAVE A PLAN.
OF COURSE I HAVE A PLAN.

CATASTROPHE AVERTED!
GREAT, LET'S GO.

WHY ARE WE LEAVING THE RIVER? THERE'S FRESH WATER AND FISH FOR US TO SURVIVE ON.
IF ANYONE COMES LOOKING FOR US, WON'T THEY LOOK THERE?
THAT'D BE THE BEST COURSE OF ACTION UNDER NORMAL CIRCUMSTANCES. UNFORTUNATELY, THE PEOPLE MOST LIKELY TO COME LOOKING FOR US ARE SPYDER.

THEN SHOULDN'T WE AT LEAST BE HEADING DOWNSTREAM? THAT'D BE THE FASTEST WAY TO CIVILIZATION.
TRUE. BUT SPYDER KNOWS THAT AS WELL. THEIR FIRST REACTION WILL BE TO CUT OFF THAT ESCAPE ROUTE, SO WE'RE GOING TO TRICK THEM BY DOUBLING BACK THE WAY WE CAME.

WAIT. THEY'LL PROBABLY EXPECT US TO DOUBLE BACK. SO WHAT WE SHOULD REALLY DO IS *DOUBLE* DOUBLE BACK AND GO DOWNSTREAM.

I THOUGHT WE'D ESTABLISHED THAT I'M IN CHARGE. AND DOUBLE DOUBLING BACK IS MORONIC. WE'RE GOING THIS WAY.
SPIN!

NO. I'M NOT ASKING YOU, I'M TELLING YOU.

DAD! WAIT! THERE'S ANOTHER REASON WE'RE HEADED THIS WAY!
OH, REALLY? AND WHAT WOULD THAT BE?
THE BEARS THAT ARE FOLLOWING US.
DON'T BE ABSURD. THERE ARE NO BEARS IN THIS PART OF THE COUNTRY.

GRRRR!

GRRRR!
SPIN!

DON'T YOU EVER GET TIRED OF BEING WRONG?
ON THE COUNT OF THREE, EVERYONE RUN AS FAST AS YOU CAN.

GRRRR
GRRRR

GRRR!
YOU DON'T RUN FROM BEARS. WE NEED TO HOLD OUR GROUND AND BACK AWAY SLOWLY.

BACK AWAY SLOWLY? WE'RE NOT TRYING TO ESCAPE TURTLES HERE.

YOU CAN'T RUN FASTER THAN A BEAR.
OF COURSE I CAN. WHERE ON EARTH DID YOU EVER HEAR THAT GARBAGE?

THE CIA AGENTS' MANUAL.

THERE'S A SECTION ON *BEARS* IN THE CIA AGENTS' MANUAL?
THERE'S A SECTION ON *EVERYTHING* IN THE CIA AGENTS' MANUAL. I'M NOT SURPRISED YOU HAVEN'T READ IT, THOUGH. THERE'S A LOT OF BIG WORDS IN IT.

AND WHAT DO WE DO IF THEY COME AFTER US?
FIRST WE TRY TO FIGHT THEM OFF—AND IF THAT DOESN'T WORK, WE PLAY DEAD.

PLAY DEAD? THAT CAN'T BE RIGHT.

COULD YOU KEEP YOUR VOICE DOWN? IT'S AGITATING THE BEARS.

THE BEARS ARE *ALREADY* AGITATED. AND IF WE PLAY DEAD, WE'RE JUST GOING TO LOOK LIKE A BUFFET TO THEM.

WE NEED TO RUN. NOW. BEFORE THEY GET MUCH CLOSER.
DAD, FOR ONCE IN YOUR LIFE, PLEASE LISTEN TO ME...

STAY AWAY FROM US!
?
AAAAAAHHH!!

YOU DON'T WANT TO EAT ME!
I'M ALL SKIN AND BONES!
TRIP!

CRACK!

WHIZZ!

DUFF!
OWWW!

GO ON! DON'T
MAKE ME COME
AFTER YOU!

ROAR!

ROAR!

SHRUG!

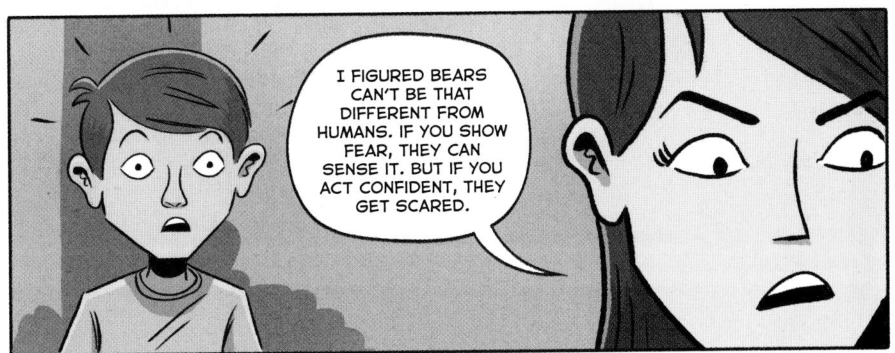
I FIGURED BEARS CAN'T BE THAT DIFFERENT FROM HUMANS. IF YOU SHOW FEAR, THEY CAN SENSE IT. BUT IF YOU ACT CONFIDENT, THEY GET SCARED.

THANK YOU. IF IT HADN'T BEEN FOR YOU... APPARENTLY YOU'RE RIGHT ABOUT ME. I REALLY AM AN UTTER SCREWUP.

THAT'S NOT COMPLETELY TRUE. YOU WERE QUITE GOOD AT PLAYING DEAD.
I WAS?

YES. THOUGH I SUPPOSE IT WASN'T MUCH OF A STRETCH.
AFTER ALL, YOUR BRAIN'S BEEN DEAD FOR YEARS.
SAG!

LATER...

FUNGI?

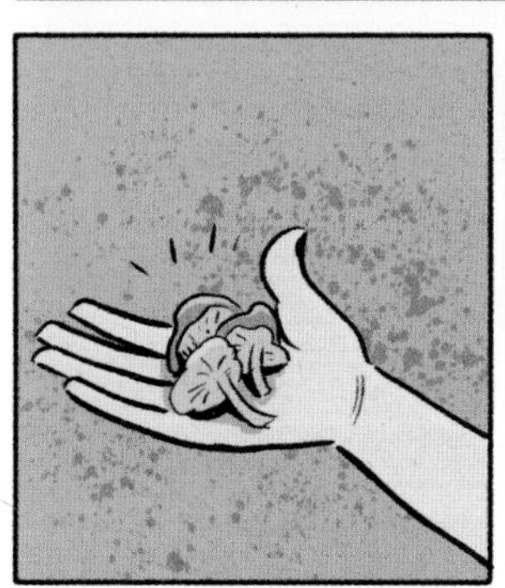

RUMBLE!

THANKS.

I THINK YOUR FATHER COULD USE A BIT OF ENCOURAGEMENT.

FEEL FREE TO GIVE IT TO HIM.

I MEANT FROM YOU.
WHY ARE YOU SO ANGRY AT HIM?
I DON'T WANT TO TALK ABOUT IT.

DO YOU HAVE ANY IDEA WHERE WE'RE GOING?
I HAVE MORE THAN AN IDEA. I KNOW *EXACTLY* WHERE WE'RE GOING.

EVEN WITHOUT A GLOBAL POSITIONING SYSTEM?

PEOPLE MANAGED TO SURVIVE FOR A LONG TIME WITHOUT GPS. THEY USED THESE THINGS CALLED *MAPS*.

WHEN I HEARD WE WERE COMING OUT HERE, I GRABBED EVERY MAP OF THE AREA I COULD FIND. SPY CAMP HAD A LARGE CACHE OF THEM.

SO WHERE ARE THEY?
BACK ON THE BUS. I DIDN'T EXACTLY HAVE TIME TO PACK DURING THE AMBUSH. BUT I DID SPEND THE WHOLE RIDE MEMORIZING THEM.

FROM WHAT I CAN TELL, WE'RE ON THE EASTERN RIDGE OF MOUNT SUKOFF.
THERE OUGHT TO BE AN ABANDONED FIRE TOWER A MILE AND A HALF THAT WAY.

YOU MEMORIZED THE MAPS? DO YOU HAVE A PHOTOGRAPHIC MEMORY?

I THINK THE CORRECT TERM IS *PERFECT RECALL*. AND NO, I CAN'T REMEMBER EVERYTHING I SEE. JUST CERTAIN THINGS.
LIKE WHAT?
MAPS, PHOTOS, BOOKS.

YOU CAN REMEMBER ENTIRE *BOOKS?*

YOU CAN'T?
NO!
BUMMER. IT SURE MAKES STUDYING FOR TESTS EASIER.

IT'S ABOUT TIME YOU GOT HERE. C'MON. NO TIME TO DILLYDALLY. WE STILL HAVE A LOT OF GROUND TO COVER.

PLEASE, JUST GIVE ME FIVE MINUTES TO REST.

WE'VE ALREADY SQUANDERED ENOUGH TIME. EVERY MINUTE WE WASTE IS A MINUTE SPYDER GETS CLOSER TO US.
IF YOU WANT TO LIE THERE IN THE OPEN WITH THE ENEMY SNIPERS ABOUT, THAT'S YOUR DECISION, BUT WE'RE MOVING ON.
SNIPERS?!

WAIT FOR ME!!!

DOES THE CIA HAVE SOME SORT OF EXPERT ON SPYDER?
YES. *YOU.*
ME? HOW COULD *I* BE THE EXPERT? I'VE ONLY HAD ONE CONVERSATION WITH A SPYDER AGENT.

WHICH IS ONE MORE CONVERSATION THAN ANYONE ELSE AT THE CIA HAS HAD. VIRTUALLY EVERYTHING THE CIA KNOWS ABOUT SPYDER IS WHAT MURRAY TOLD YOU.
IN FACT, THAT CONVERSATION WAS THE FIRST PROOF THE CIA EVER GOT THAT SPYDER REALLY EXISTS.

SO WHEN THE CIA SAYS THEY'RE TRYING TO PROTECT ME FROM SPYDER... THEY DON'T EVEN KNOW WHO THAT IS?
EXACTLY.
DO YOU THINK THE CIA EVEN KNOWS WHERE WE ARE?

NO. BUT THAT'S WHY WE'RE HEADING *THERE*.

THE FOREST SERVICE USED TO POST MEN UP HERE TO KEEP AN EYE OUT FOR FIRES.
NOW THEY DO THAT WITH SATELLITES, SO THEY'VE PROBABLY FORGOTTEN THIS PLACE EVEN EXISTS.

WAIT. WHAT IF SPYDER HAS SET UP AN AMBUSH?

THAT'S A RISK I'M WILLING TO TAKE. WE NEED TO ESTABLISH CONTACT WITH THE CIA.
PERHAPS NOT. THEY'VE ACTIVATED KLONDIKE.

WHEN?
SPIN!

A FEW DAYS AGO.
?

WHY DIDN'T ANYONE TELL ME?

BECAUSE YOU'RE A TEENAGER. ONLY AGENTS WITH TOP SECURITY CLEARANCE WERE SUPPOSED TO KNOW.

WHAT'S KLONDIKE?
A VERY BAD IDEA.

CRACK!

CREAK!

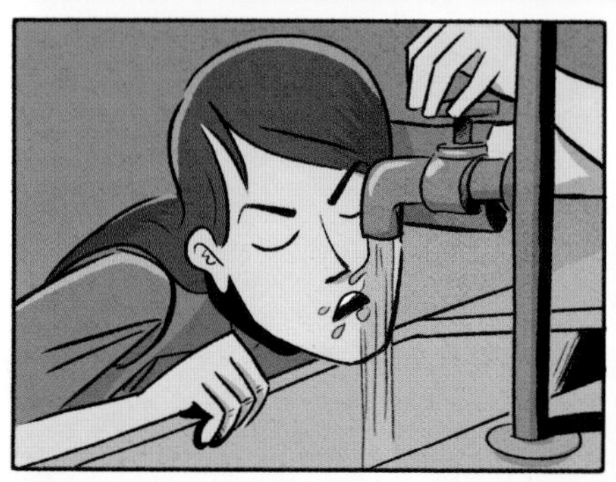

THIS IS RAINWATER. IT'S FRESH AND GOOD.
WIPE

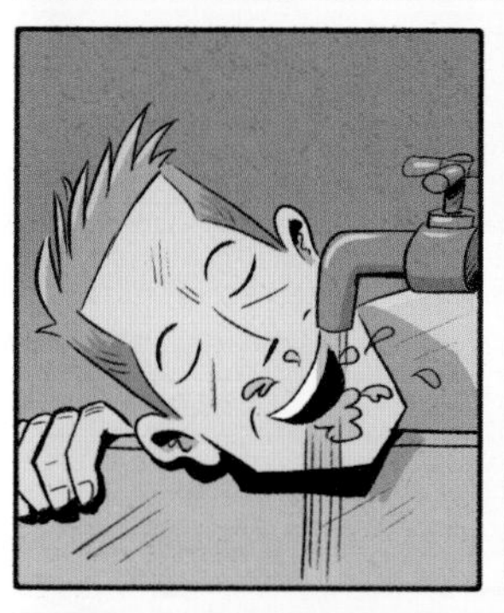

AHH!
AHH!

WIND!

GRAB!

MAYDAY. THIS IS AGENT 2364, CODE NAME BIG DOG, CALLING FOR EMERGENCY BACKUP.

HELLO, AGENT HALE! WE'VE BEEN HOPING TO HEAR FROM YOU!

IT'S GOOD TO HEAR YOUR VOICE AS WELL.
WHAT'S YOUR LOCATION?

GRAB!

WHAT'S YOUR SECURITY CLEARANCE CODE?

AH. THIS MUST BE THE FAMOUS ERICA HALE. I KNEW WE COULDN'T TRICK *YOU* WITH A SIMPLE RUSE.

WAIT. SO YOU'RE NOT THE CIA?

NO. I'M WITH SPYDER. IS BEN RIPLEY THERE WITH YOU TOO?

NO. WE WERE SEPARATED FROM BEN IN THE RIVER. WE THINK HE GOT WASHED FARTHER DOWNSTREAM.
WELL, YOU'D BETTER TRACK HIM DOWN. WE NEED YOU TO BRING HIM TO US.
AND WHY WOULD I WANT TO DO THAT?

BECAUSE WE'VE CAPTURED A FEW OF HIS FRIENDS. AND WE'LL KILL THEM IF YOU DON'T.

ARE YOU STILL THERE? HELLO? ERICA? HELLO?

I'M HERE. BUT I'M WONDERING IF YOU'RE TELLING ME THE TRUTH.

YOU THINK I'M LYING ABOUT THE HOSTAGES?

YOU GUYS AREN'T EXACTLY KNOWN FOR YOUR HONESTY.

TOUCHÉ. HOW'S THIS FOR PROOF?

ERICA? IS THAT YOU?
YES, IT'S ME. HOW ARE THEY TREATING YOU?
ALL RIGHT, I GUESS. THEY HAVEN'T TORTURED US OR ANYTHING. WARREN'S BEEN CRYING A LOT, BUT OTHER THAN THAT, I GUESS WE'RE OKAY.

WHAT ABOUT EVERYONE ELSE WHO WAS ON THE BUS?

I DON'T KNOW. I GUESS THEY'RE ALL STILL BACK IN THE WILDERNESS. SPYDER ONLY TOOK US.
ZOE, HOW MANY SPYDER AGENTS ARE THERE?
I DON'T KNOW. THEY HAVE US BLINDFOLDED. ALTHOUGH I'VE RECOGNIZED AT LEAST FOUR DIFFERENT VOICES.

THAT'S ENOUGH OF THAT. NOW, HERE'S HOW THINGS WILL PLAY OUT: AT THE INTERSECTION OF VIRGINIA STATE ROUTES 522 AND 37, THERE IS A FARM WITH A LARGE RED BARN.
WE WILL BE AT THAT BARN WITH YOUR FRIENDS IN EXACTLY SIX HOURS. IF YOU ARE NOT THERE WITH BEN RIPLEY AT THAT TIME, WE WILL KILL THE FIRST HOSTAGE–

WHOA–SIX HOURS? LET'S BE REASONABLE HERE.
I'M TRYING TO.

MAP

SIX HOURS ISN'T ANYWHERE CLOSE TO REASONABLE. FIRST OF ALL, I DON'T KNOW WHERE BEN IS.
HE COULD HAVE WASHED HALFWAY TO WASHINGTON, DC, FOR ALL I KNOW.

DON'T JERK ME AROUND. BEN'S STANDING RIGHT BESIDE YOU, ISN'T HE?

HE'S NOT. SIX HOURS JUST ISN'T GOING TO FLY. I NEED SIX DAYS.

THAT'S UNACCEPTABLE. WE'LL GIVE YOU TWO DAYS, AND THAT'S OUR FINAL OFFER.

AND IT GOES WITHOUT SAYING THAT BRINGING MR. RIPLEY IS NONNEGOTIABLE.

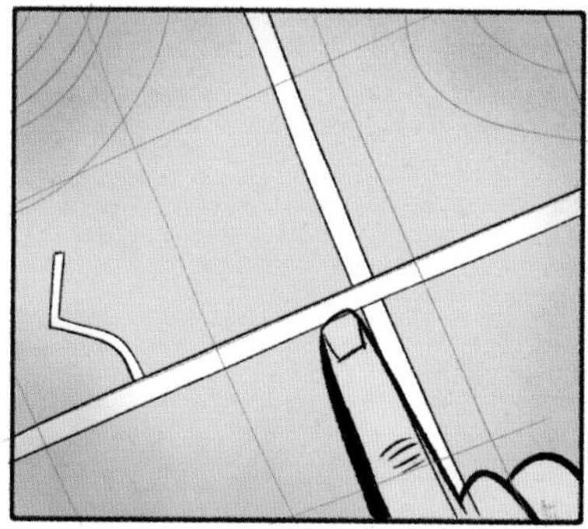

COULDN'T YOU ACCEPT ME IN HIS PLACE? I'M A MUCH BETTER SPY.

WINK!
THAT'S A TEMPTING OFFER.

BUT THE FACT IS, BEN HAS SOME VERY SPECIAL ABILITIES THAT YOU DON'T. ABILITIES THAT HE MIGHT NOT EVEN BE AWARE HE HAS.
THAT'S ENOUGH TALK. WE'LL SEE YOU IN TWO DAYS.

CLICK!

COME ON. WE NEED TO GET MOVING.

HOW COULD SPYDER KNOW I HAVE THESE ABILITIES WHEN I DON'T EVEN KNOW WHAT THEY ARE?
MURRAY HILL. HE WAS OBVIOUSLY STUDYING YOU VERY CLOSELY WHILE HE WAS WORKING AS A MOLE.

HOW HARD IS IT GOING TO BE FOR US TO MAKE IT TO THE HOSTAGE SWAP IN TWO DAYS?

OH, NOT HARD AT ALL. IT'S NOT REALLY THAT FAR. I WAS BLUFFING. WE COULD EASILY BE THERE IN A DAY IF WE HAD TO.

THEN WHY DID YOU ASK FOR TWO?

BECAUSE WE'RE NOT GOING THERE RIGHT AWAY. WE HAVE ONE OTHER PLACE TO VISIT BEFORE THAT.
AND THAT'S WHY WE'RE IN SUCH A HURRY?
NO, WE'RE IN SUCH A HURRY SO WE CAN EVACUATE THE FIRE TOWER BEFORE SPYDER ATTACKS IT.

HOW LONG DO YOU THINK WE HAVE UNTIL THEY GET HERE?
WIPE
THAT DEPENDS ON WHAT THEY'RE SENDING AFTER US. IF IT'S AN ASSAULT TEAM, IT MIGHT BE HALF AN HOUR...

WOOSH!

BOOM!

SCHWANG!

CRASH!

DID YOU SAY WE HAVE ONE OTHER PLACE TO VISIT BEFORE YOU TRADE ME FOR THE HOSTAGES?
YES.
WHERE?
ISN'T IT OBVIOUS? WE HAVE TO FIND OUT IF MURRAY HILL IS REALLY AT APPLE VALLEY OR NOT.

DO YOU SMELL SMOKE?

C'MON, THIS WAY!

WHY IS IT SO IMPORTANT TO INVESTIGATE MURRAY RIGHT NOW? SHOULDN'T RESCUING THE OTHERS BE OUR PRIORITY?
NO, TAKING SPYDER DOWN IS THE PRIORITY. WE HAVE TO FIGURE OUT WHAT THEY'RE UP TO. WHY DO THEY NEED YOU SO BADLY?
AND WHAT'S GOING ON WITH MURRAY HILL?

I HAVE A HUNCH THAT MURRAY IS THE KEY TO ALL OF THIS. AND IF WE CAN LEARN WHAT SPYDER'S PLANS ARE, THEN MAYBE WE WON'T HAVE TO EXCHANGE YOU FOR YOUR FRIENDS AFTER ALL.
SOUNDS GOOD.
ONE MORE THING. DON'T TELL ANYONE ANYTHING ABOUT WHAT'S GOING ON HERE.

I'M NOT SURE THAT'S THE BEST POLICY. IF WE CONTACT THE RIGHT PEOPLE AT THE CIA, THEY COULD HELP US RESCUE YOUR FRIENDS.
AS FAR AS WE KNOW, SPYDER IS MONITORING ALL COMMUNICATION WITH THE CIA RIGHT NOW. THERE'S NO WAY WE CAN CONTACT THE AGENCY WITHOUT SPYDER KNOWING.

YOU'RE AWFUL FAR FROM CIVILIZATION! WHAT WERE Y'ALL DOING WAY OUT HERE?

HIKING!

Y'ALL KNOW WHAT STARTED THAT FIRE?

IT WAS AN ENEMY MISSILE! I WORK FOR THE CIA AND—OOF!
DUFF!

UNFORTUNATELY, MY FATHER WAS STRUCK ON THE HEAD BY A PIECE OF BURNING DEBRIS. HE'S BEEN TALKING CRAZY EVER SINCE. HE'S NOT IN THE CIA. HE'S AN ORTHODONTIST.
DON'T WORRY! WE'LL GET YOUR DADDY MEDICAL HELP AS SOON AS WE LAND.

HOW'S YOUR HEAD, SIR?

MY HEAD IS FINE. IT'S THE SAFETY OF OUR COUNTRY THAT'S IN JEOPARDY. I NEED TO CALL THE CIA IMMEDIATELY!
HE'S BEEN SAYING THINGS LIKE THIS EVER SINCE THAT DEBRIS HIT HIM.

SOMETIMES, A TRAUMATIC EXPERIENCE CAN CAUSE TEMPORARY DELUSIONS IN PEOPLE. WE'LL TAKE GOOD CARE OF HIM.

I AM NOT DELUSIONAL! I AM A HIGHLY DECORATED CIA AGENT!
OF COURSE YOU ARE. I'M SURE YOU'VE SAVED THE WORLD SEVERAL TIMES.

I'M ALEXANDER HALE!!

THIS REALLY ISN'T NECESSARY!

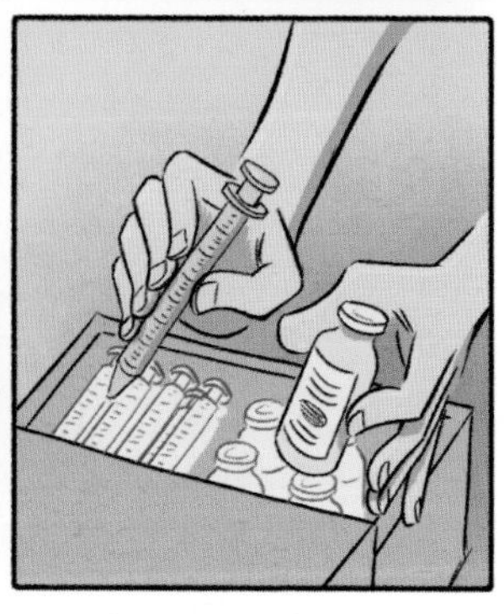

YOU DON'T UNDERSTAND!
CLICK!

THIS IS A MISTAKE!

I AM AGENT ALEXANDER HA– YOW!

DID YOU JUST STICK ME WITH SOMETHING?

I THINK IT WAS A MOSQUITO.
SLAP!
OUCH, ONE JUST GOT ME, TOO.

YOU *DID* GIVE ME SOMETHING.

HOW DARE YOU, ERICA? I'M YOUR...YOUR... FATHHHHPPBBLE.
PAT PAT!

VICEROY MEDICAL CLINIC
WARDENSVILLE, WEST VIRGINIA

EMERGENCY ROOM

IT'S ALWAYS LIKE THIS AT THE BEGINNING OF SUMMER VACATION.
IS THIS YOUR FATHER?
YES...
I'M ALEXANDURBLE PURBLE...HUP!

WILL HE BE OKAY?

DON'T WORRY, DEAR. YOUR FATHER IS MERELY DELUSIONAL. BUT GIVEN THE OTHER THINGS WE HAVE TO DEAL WITH IN THIS PLACE, IT MIGHT BE A WHILE UNTIL WE CAN SEE HIM.

SOB!

WIPE!

GRAB MY DAD'S FEET. WE'RE GETTING OUT OF HERE.

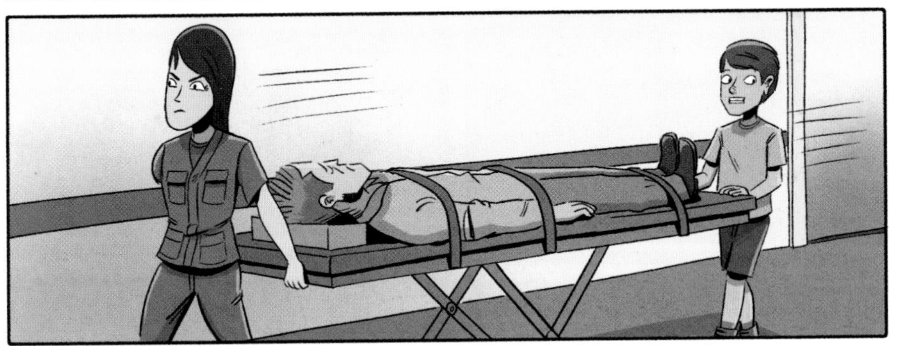

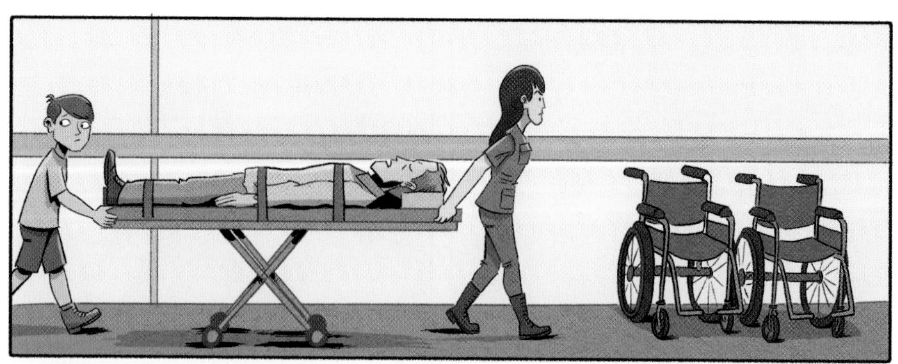

REHABILITATI
CENTER

YOU'RE STEALING THIS CAR?
BORROWING IT. TEMPORARILY.

I KNOW IT'S NOT EXACTLY THE STAUNCH MORAL THING TO DO, BUT LIKE DAD SAID, OUR COUNTRY'S SAFETY IS IN JEOPARDY.

VICEROY MEDICAL CLINIC
WARDENSVILLE, WEST VIRGINIA

ONE WAY
REMEMBER WHERE MURRAY IS INCARCERATED?
THE APPLE VALLEY REFORMATION CENTER FOR DELINQUENT TEENS.
RIGHT. IT'S LOCATED NEAR A TOWN CALLED VAUGHN, VIRGINIA. IS THERE A MAP IN THIS CAR?

WEST VIRGINI STAT

LOOKS LIKE IT'S ABOUT AN HOUR AWAY.
zZZZZ

DO YOU THINK SPYDER KNOWS WE SURVIVED THE MISSILE ATTACK?

DEFINITELY. THERE'S NO QUESTION THEY DO.

WHY DO YOU SAY THAT?

BECAUSE THEY WEREN'T TRYING TO KILL US.

THEY LAUNCHED A MISSILE AT US!
BUT THEY GAVE US TIME TO ESCAPE. IT'S A WARNING. THEY ONLY LAUNCHED THE MISSILE TO LET US KNOW THEY MEAN BUSINESS.

WARDENSVILLE CITY LIMITS

Welcome to
Vaughn

MOTEL
SUNRISE MOTEL

KEEP AN EYE ON MY FATHER. I'LL GET US A ROOM.
ZZZZ
WE DON'T HAVE ANY MONEY.

YOU DON'T HAVE ANY MONEY. I DO.

WHERE'D YOU GET THAT?
OUR PARAMEDICS.
YOU PICKPOCKETED THEM?

I HAD TO, BEN. THIS IS A CRISIS.

MOTEL
OPEN

THE MANAGER LET ME HAVE IT. I TOLD HIM WE NEEDED TO PUT THE BUMPER BACK ON.
WHAT'S IT REALLY FOR?

ISN'T IT OBVIOUS? SECURITY.

FIVE MINUTES LATER...

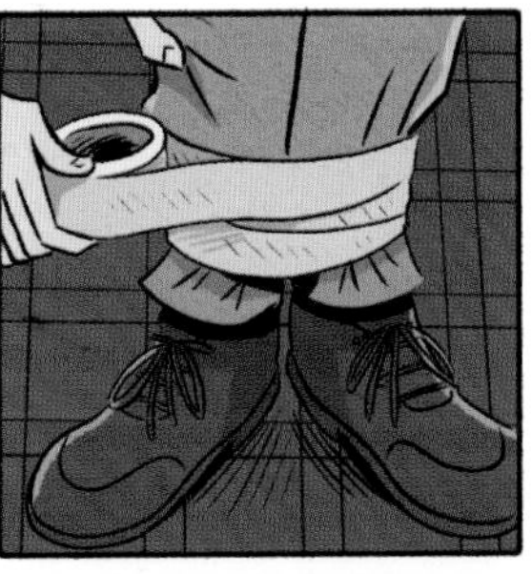

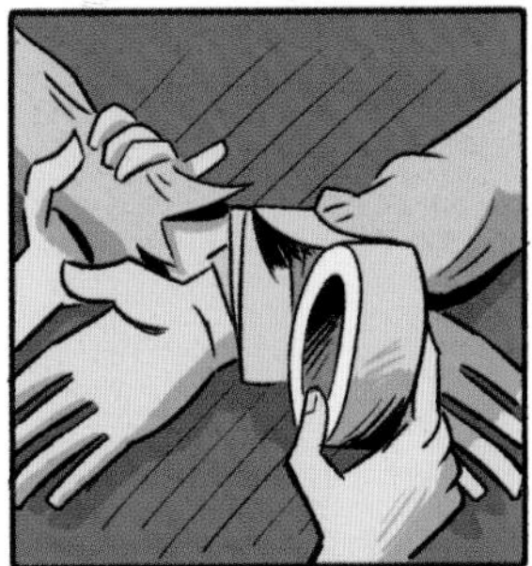

I'M GOING OUT TO SURVEY APPLE VALLEY. I'LL BE BACK LATER.
CAN'T I COME? YOUR FATHER'S NOT GOING ANYWHERE.
NO, BUT HE COULD STILL BE A PROBLEM.

I COULD GO DO THE RECONNAISSANCE, AND YOU COULD STAY HERE WITH YOUR FATHER, GET SOME REST, AND, UH...
WORK OUT ANY ISSUES THAT YOU TWO MIGHT HAVE.

DO YOU HAVE ANY IDEA HOW TO INFILTRATE A PENAL INSTITUTION WITH LEVEL-FOUR SECURITY?
NOT EXACTLY.

AND THAT'S WHY *I'M* DOING THE RECON.
I SHOULDN'T BE TOO LONG.

SLAM!

zzzzzzZZ
ZZZZZZZZ

ERRRGH!

URRGH!

4:00AM

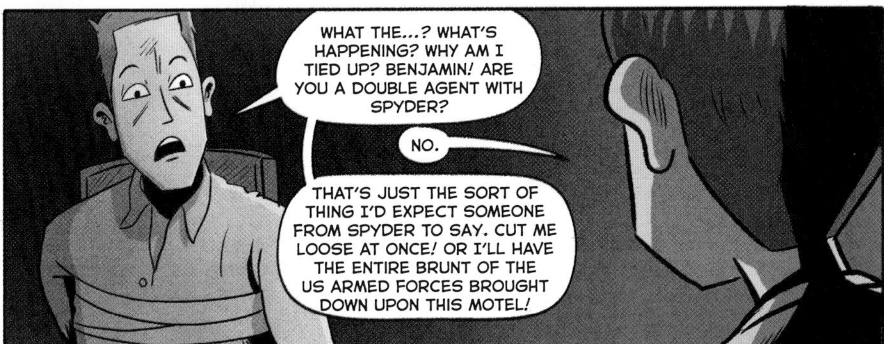
WHAT THE...? WHAT'S HAPPENING? WHY AM I TIED UP? BENJAMIN! ARE YOU A DOUBLE AGENT WITH SPYDER?
NO.
THAT'S JUST THE SORT OF THING I'D EXPECT SOMEONE FROM SPYDER TO SAY. CUT ME LOOSE AT ONCE! OR I'LL HAVE THE ENTIRE BRUNT OF THE US ARMED FORCES BROUGHT DOWN UPON THIS MOTEL!

ALEXANDER, I KNOW THAT'S NOT TRUE. AND I'M NOT A DOUBLE AGENT. I'M ON YOUR SIDE.
THEN WHY HAVE YOU TAPED ME TO A CHAIR?
IT WAS ERICA'S IDEA. SHE FELT YOU'D CAUSE LESS TROUBLE THIS WAY.

WHY WOULD SHE THINK THAT?

MAYBE BECAUSE YOU'VE CHALLENGED HER AUTHORITY AND LIED AT EVERY TURN. SHE SAYS YOU'RE A FRAUD.
AND YOU BELIEVE THAT?

YOU DID STEAL THE CREDIT FOR CAPTURING MURRAY FROM ME.

IF I'M HONEST, WILL YOU SET ME FREE?

NO. ERICA WOULD KILL ME.
WHY IS SHE SO ANGRY AT YOU?

A FEW WEEKS AGO, I SORT OF LOST A BRIEFCASE FULL OF IMPORTANT CLASSIFIED DOCUMENTS.
CLOSED
CLASSIFIED
YUMMY BURGER
YB
HOW? DID THE ENEMY STEAL IT?

ER...NO. I THINK I LEFT IT IN—WELL, IT DOESN'T MATTER.

ANYWAY, IT WOULDN'T HAVE LOOKED GOOD IF I'D SIMPLY ADMITTED THE TRUTH. SO I KIND OF BLAMED IT ON ERICA.
I TOLD THE TOP BRASS SHE'D SPILLED A GLASS OF MILK ON THE DOCUMENTS AND DESTROYED THEM.

AND WHAT DID THE TOP BRASS DO?

THEY, UH...THEY PUT A BLACK MARK ON ERICA'S SCHOOL RECORDS.
WHICH MEANS WHAT?

HER CHANCES OF GOING INTO THE FIELD AFTER GRADUATION ARE, ER... SEVERELY DIMINISHED.

I DIDN'T REALIZE THEY WOULD DING HER! I THOUGHT THEY'D LET IT SLIDE.

YOU THOUGHT NO SUCH THING.

SWEETHEART, I TOLD YOU I WAS SORRY...
AND I TOLD YOU NOT TO CALL ME "SWEETHEART."
OR "KITTEN."
OR ANYTHING ELSE CUTE AND FAMILIAL.

IF YOU'RE GOING TO PUT YOUR CAREER BEFORE ME, YOU DON'T GET TO ACT LIKE MY FATHER.

IT WAS A SIMPLE MISTAKE. I'M WORKING ON CLEANING IT UP. IT'S MY NUMBER ONE PRIORITY.

OBVIOUSLY, THAT'S A LIE. BECAUSE IF IT *WAS* YOUR NUMBER ONE PRIORITY, YOU'D HAVE ALREADY ADMITTED THE TRUTH ABOUT WHAT HAPPENED.

SWISH!

SLICE!

YOU'RE CUTTING ME FREE?
UNFORTUNATELY, WE NEED YOU.
SLICE!

AH. SEE? I'M NOT AS INCOMPETENT AS YOU SAY.

NO, YOU ARE. WE DON'T NEED YOU FOR ANY SPY SKILLS. WE NEED YOU BECAUSE YOU'RE OLD.
APPLE VALLEY WON'T LET US IN UNLESS WE'RE ACCOMPANIED BY AN ADULT.
SPIN!

THERE ARE A FEW STIPULATIONS TO YOUR RELEASE, HOWEVER...
YOU ADMIT THAT I AM IN CHARGE. YOU ONLY DO WHAT I TELL YOU TO.
AND YOU NEVER SPEAK UNLESS I SAY SO.

SAG!

AND FINALLY: WHEN THIS IS ALL OVER, YOU CALL THE HEAD OF THE CIA HIMSELF AND ADMIT WHAT YOU DID TO ME.
FINE.

OKAY THEN. LET'S GET TO THE BOTTOM OF THIS MURRAY HILL BUSINESS.

APPLE VALLEY
REFORMATION CAMP FOR DELINQUENT TEENS

Celeb Weekly

THE NAME'S ALEXANDER HALE. CIA AGENT NUMBER 2364. I'M HERE TO SEE ONE OF YOUR INMATES. A MURRAY HILL.
MURRAY! OH, HE'S SUCH A SWEETIE!

UM, ARE YOU DELIVERING THESE CHILDREN HERE FOR INCARCERATION?
NO, THESE ARE *MY* CHILDREN. TODAY'S TAKE YOUR KIDS TO WORK DAY AT THE CIA.

OOH, THAT'S ADORABLE! GO ON THROUGH.
PUSH!

THANKS TO MY RECONNAISSANCE LAST NIGHT, I LEARNED THAT THIS PLACE ACTUALLY HAS A SECURITY LEVEL OF NEGATIVE THREE.

HOW CAN THEY KEEP A CRIMINAL AS BAD AS MURRAY HILL HERE? THIS ISN'T PUNISHMENT. IT'S LIKE SENDING HIM TO A SPA FOR FIVE YEARS.
MURRAY IS ONLY FOURTEEN. THERE AREN'T A LOT OF MAXIMUM-SECURITY OPTIONS FOR TEENAGERS.

THANKS FOR COMING TO SEE US AT APPLE VALLEY! I UNDERSTAND YOU'RE HERE TO SEE MURRAY.
I'VE ALREADY ARRANGED FOR HIM TO BE BROUGHT TO OUR VISITATION CENTER.

WOULD EITHER OF YOU LIKE A LOLLIPOP?

DUE TO THE NATURE OF HIS CRIMES, WE HAVE TO KEEP HIM UNDER A BIT TIGHTER REIN THAN MOST OF OUR OTHER GUESTS HERE.

MURRAY LIVES IN OUR HIGH-SECURITY WING.

THERE HE IS! OUR MURRAY!

PAT
PAT!

WE HERE AT APPLE VALLEY STRONGLY BELIEVE IN "REFORMATION THROUGH CONTEMPLATION."
ALTHOUGH MURRAY IS A BIT OF A SPECIAL CASE.

UH...THAT'S NOT MURRAY.

IT'S NOT?
YOU DON'T KNOW? THAT'S FUNNY. I THOUGHT YOU CAPTURED HIM.

AS FAR AS I KNOW, THAT IS MURRAY HILL.
THAT'S WHAT THE GOVERNMENT AGENTS WHO BROUGHT HIM HERE TOLD ME.
BUT YOU NEVER CHECKED TO MAKE SURE?

HOW WOULD I DO THAT?

RUN HIS FINGERPRINTS. OR MAYBE LOOK UP A PHOTO OF MURRAY HILL IN THE CIA DATABASE.
YOU'RE NOT AMISH, RIGHT? YOU'VE GOT A COMPUTER HERE?

WHY SHOULD IT EVEN OCCUR TO ANYONE TO DO SUCH A THING? THE CIA DROPPED HIM OFF HERE.
THEY TOLD ME HE WAS MURRAY HILL. AM I SUPPOSED TO QUESTION THE CIA?
FAN FAN!
YES. DID YOU EVEN CHECK TO SEE IF THE AGENTS HAD OFFICIAL ID WHEN THEY DROPPED THIS KID OFF? BECAUSE NO ONE CHECKED OURS JUST NOW.

THIS IS LUDICROUS. IF THAT BOY ISN'T MURRAY HILL, WHY DIDN'T HE EVER SAY ANYTHING?
ARE YOU SUGGESTING HE WILLINGLY TOOK THE PLACE OF A PRISONER?

WHAT DID SPYDER OFFER YOU TO TAKE MURRAY'S PLACE?
I DON'T KNOW WHO SPYDER IS.
GRAB!

DON'T PLAY DUMB WITH US.
I DON'T THINK HE'S PLAYING. I THINK HE REALLY IS DUMB.

DID *SOMEONE* OFFER YOU SOMETHING TO COME HERE?
A HUNDRED THOUSAND DOLLARS.

THAT'S IT? MURRAY'S SENTENCE WAS FIVE YEARS! YOU ALLOWED YOURSELF TO BE INCARCERATED FOR ONLY TWENTY-THOUSAND DOLLARS A YEAR?
SLAP!

STILL SEEMS LIKE A WHOLE LOT OF MONEY TO ME.
AND THIS PLACE IS A HECK OF A LOT NICER THAN THE JUVENILE HALL WHERE THEY FOUND ME.

IT SEEMS OUR FRIENDS AT SPYDER OUTWITTED THE CIA YET AGAIN.
ONCE THEY FOUND OUT THAT MURRAY HAD BEEN ASSIGNED TO THIS LAME FACILITY, THEY FOUND A DUPE AT SOME JUVIE HALL, SPRANG HIM, AND SWAPPED HIM OUT FOR MURRAY.
BUT HOW?
HA HA HA!

THE EASIEST WAY WOULD BE TO CORRUPT THE AGENTS WHO WERE SUPPOSED TO DELIVER MURRAY HERE.

WHATEVER THE CASE, APPLE VALLEY'S BEEN BABYSITTING THE WRONG GUY FOR FIVE MONTHS WHILE THE REAL MURRAY'S BEEN FREE AS A BIRD.
HA HA HA!
HA HA HA!

MURRAY HILL *WANTED* ME TO SEE HIM THE OTHER DAY. HE WANTED US TO KNOW HE WAS OUT. THEREFORE, HE MUST HAVE WANTED US TO FIGURE OUT HOW HE'D DONE IT.

AND SINCE SPYDER IS ALWAYS ONE STEP AHEAD OF US...
THEY PROBABLY EXPECTED THAT WE'D COME HERE.

BEEP
BEEP!
SWING!
HA HA
HA!!
SURPRISE!!!

SLAM!

HA HA HA!

SLIDE!
HAHA!
CRASH!
CREECH!
E-GO THIS WAY
K.

RIP!
E- GO THIS WAY
K.
RIP!
E- GO THIS WAY
POTTERY STUDIO
E- GO

WHO'S THAT FROM?
A FRIEND.
IT'S DG-7. A LIQUID-POLYMER GREASE.
RIP!
THE NAVY DESIGNED IT TO LUBRICATE AIRCRAFT ENGINES...
2
SQUEEZE!
WHOOOAA!!
...ALTHOUGH...
...IT'S ALSO VERY EFFECTIVE FOR TAKING OUT YOUR ENEMIES.

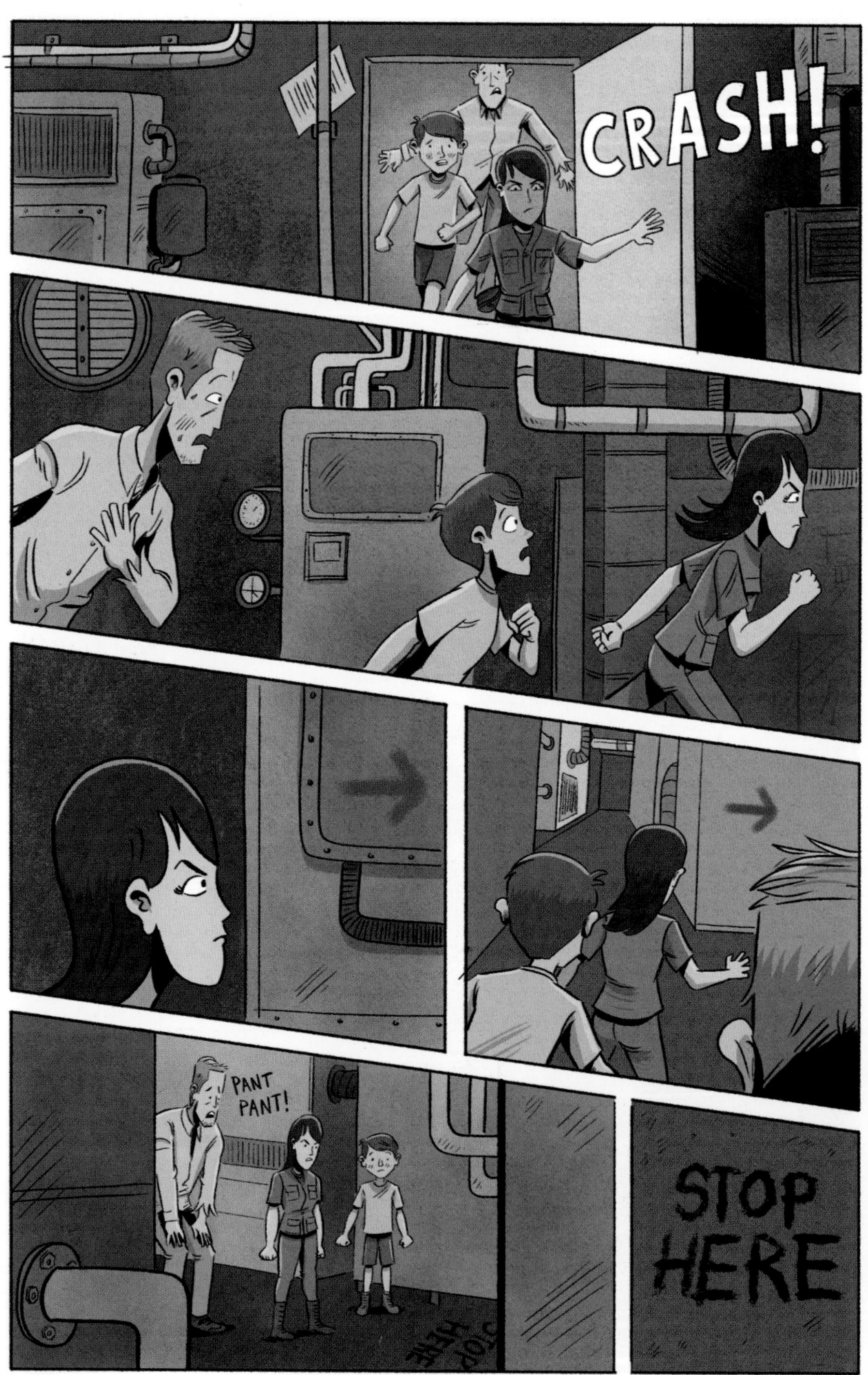
CRASH!
PANT PANT!
STOP HERE
STOP HERE

STOP
HERE

STOP
HERE

WOOSH!
THUMP!
CRACK!
WHACK!
BOFF!
SPIN!
SMACK!

CRACK!
UURGH.
UUUURGH.
ERRRGH.
DON'T WORRY. YOU'RE ALL SAFE NOW.

HI, GRANDPA.

GRANDPA, THIS IS BEN RIPLEY. BEN, THIS IS MY GRANDFATHER, CYRUS HALE.
AKA AGENT KLONDIKE.

YOU'D BETTER BE WORTH ALL THE TROUBLE WE'VE GONE THROUGH FOR YOU.
URGH.

GULP!

WHAT DO YOU WANT WITH THIS KID?
THERE ARE A LOT MORE OF US COMING, OLD MAN. I'M NOT SAYING SQUAT TO YOU.

HE'S NOT BLUFFING. LISTEN.

STOMP!
STOMP!
STOMP!
STOMP!
STOMP!
STOMP!

DAGNABBIT. COME ON, FOLLOW ME.

THERE'S NO POINT IN RUNNING! THIS VALLEY'S A DEAD END. WE'VE GOT YOU CORNERED!
WE'LL SEE ABOUT THAT.

I DON'T SUPPOSE WE COULD SLOW THINGS DOWN A NOTCH? I'VE GOT A STITCH IN MY SIDE.
SOUNDS LIKE SOMEONE OUGHT TO BE SPENDING A LITTLE LESS TIME SNOWING HIS SUPERIORS AND A LITTLE MORE TIME AT THE GYM.

I'M IN PERFECTLY GOOD SHAPE, DAD! THIS IS JUST A RESIDUAL INJURY FROM MY LAST MISSION. A TERRORIST IN AFGHANISTAN TRIED TO WAYLAY ME WITH A MONKEY WRENCH...

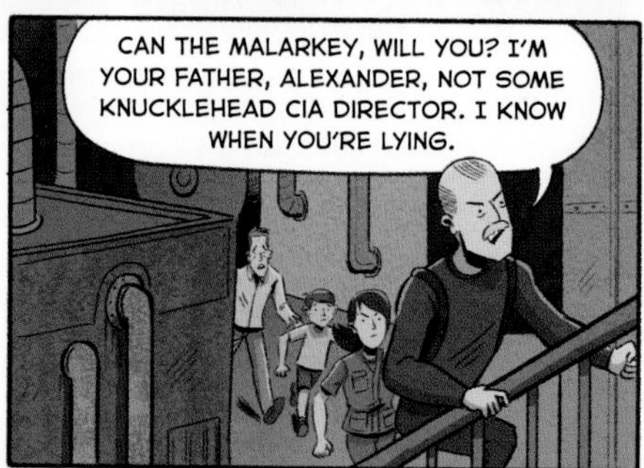
CAN THE MALARKEY, WILL YOU? I'M YOUR FATHER, ALEXANDER, NOT SOME KNUCKLEHEAD CIA DIRECTOR. I KNOW WHEN YOU'RE LYING.

Pool
Maintenance

DO YOU HAVE A GETAWAY CAR?
IT'S ABOUT AN HOUR'S HIKE.

AN HOUR?

IT'S THE BEST I COULD DO ON SHORT NOTICE. YOU REALLY PUT YOURSELF IN THE CROSSHAIRS HERE, ALEX.
YOU COULDN'T HAVE PICKED A BETTER PLACE TO BE AMBUSHED BY THE ENEMY.

IT WASN'T *MY* IDEA. IT WAS ERICA'S!

LAYING BLAME ON YOUR DAUGHTER AGAIN, ARE YOU?
HOW LONG WERE YOU TAILING US, GRANDPA?

EVER SINCE YOU GOT OFF THE HELICOPTER YESTERDAY. AND I FOLLOWED YOU ON YOUR LITTLE RECONNAISSANCE MISSION LAST NIGHT, SO I HAD A GOOD IDEA WHAT YOU WERE UP TO.
GAVE ME SOME TIME TO PLAN AN EMERGENCY ESCAPE ROUTE.

IF YOU WERE SO CONCERNED ABOUT US, WHY DIDN'T YOU STOP US *BEFORE* WE WENT TO APPLE VALLEY?

YOU'RE QUESTIONING ME? YOU, A FIRST YEAR AT THE ACADEMY. DO YOU HAVE ANY IDEA WHO I AM?
I'M SORRY. BUT...
SPIN!

I'M CYRUS HALE, FOR CRYING OUT LOUD!
I'VE BEEN SERVING THIS COUNTRY SINCE YOUR MOMMY AND DADDY WERE STILL IN DIAPERS.

I FACED DOWN THE RUSSKIES IN THE COLD WAR.

I PERSONALLY ENDED THE BAY OF PIGS FIASCO.

IF IT WASN'T FOR ME, THIS PLANET WOULD HAVE GONE THERMONUCLEAR TEN TIMES OVER....

ACTUALLY, GRANDPA, IT WASN'T A BAD QUESTION.

I SUPPOSE YOU'RE RIGHT, CUPCAKE.
FIRST, I HAD DIRECT ORDERS NOT TO ENGAGE YOU UNLESS IT WAS ABSOLUTELY NECESSARY.
PHEW!

SECOND, I FIGURED YOU MIGHT ACTUALLY LEARN SOME IMPORTANT INFORMATION ON YOUR MISSION.

WE *DID* GET SOME USEFUL INFORMATION, DIDN'T WE?
YOU DID, PRINCESS. YOU DETERMINED THAT SPYDER IS FAR MORE ENTRENCHED IN THE CIA THAN ANYONE REALIZED.
WE'D BEEN THINKING THEY HAD ONE OR TWO DOUBLE AGENTS AT MOST. BUT NOW, IT'S EVIDENT THEY HAVE FAR MORE.

LATER...

WHAT'S WRONG?
I'M JUST TRYING TO REMEMBER THE WAY TO THE CAR.

PAT PAT!

?
?
?
THE CAR'S THIS WAY.

YOU WOULDN'T HAVE TO TRY TO MEMORIZE A PATH THROUGH THE WOODS LIKE THIS IF YOU'D JUST GET A SMARTPHONE.
IF YOU HAD ONE, YOU COULD USE THE GLOBAL POSITIONING SYSTEM TO FIND THE CAR...
YOU DON'T HAVE TO TELL ME ABOUT GPS. I KNOW PLENTY ABOUT IT.

TAKE IT FROM ME, IT'S NOT AS ACCURATE AS EVERYBODY THINKS.

NOW, GRANDPA, DON'T BE SUCH A DINOSAUR. DAD'S ACTUALLY RIGHT ABOUT THIS.

THERE'S A FIRST TIME FOR EVERYTHING.

WHAT IS IT? DO I HAVE A TICK ON ME? IT'S NOT A BIG ONE, IS IT?
I'M JUST TRYING TO FIGURE OUT WHAT'S SO ALL-FIRED IMPORTANT ABOUT YOU.
SIX MONTHS AGO, WE DIDN'T EVEN KNOW FOR SURE THAT SPYDER EXISTED.

AND NOW, THEY REVEAL THEMSELVES BY COMING FOR A FIRST-YEAR STUDENT WHO'S STILL WET BEHIND THE EARS?

WHY? WHAT'S SO SPECIAL ABOUT YOU?
I DON'T KNOW.

LOOKS LIKE THEY'VE FIGURED OUT WE'VE GIVEN THEM THE SLIP.
THINK THEY'LL COME AFTER US?

NO. THEY KNOW WE HAVE TO COME SEE THEM AGAIN ANYHOW.

THEY'VE STILL GOT OUR FRIENDS CAPTIVE.
WE HAVE TO GO GET THEM.

EVEN THOUGH THAT'S EXACTLY WHAT SPYDER WANTS?
YES, BUT IT DOESN'T MEAN WE HAVE TO PLAY BY SPYDER'S RULES.
THAT'S MY GIRL.

WHAT DO YOU MEAN?
THIS TIME, WE'RE GOING TO GET THE JUMP ON *THEM*.

LATER...
TOSS!

SPYDER WILL BE WATCHING THE MAIN HIGHWAYS. BEST TO STICK TO THE BLUE ROUTES.

NOM, NOM, NOM, NOM.
YUMMY BURGER
YB

SO THIS WAS YOUR PLAN ALL ALONG? GETTING TO SPYDER A DAY EARLY?

YOU NEVER MEET THE ENEMY ON THEIR TERMS. YOU MERELY AGREE TO THEIR TERMS AND THEN CATCH THEM OFF GUARD.
WHERE WERE YOU SUPPOSED TO MAKE THE EXCHANGE?

AN OLD BARN JUST NORTH OF THE CITY, AT THE INTERSECTION OF STATE ROUTES 37 AND 522. BUT THAT'S NOT WHERE THEY'RE ACTUALLY HOLDING THE HOSTAGES.

HOW DO YOU KNOW THAT?

I SCOPED THE PLACE OUT LAST NIGHT, AFTER I DID RECON AT APPLE VALLEY.
NICE WORK, BUTTERCUP. WHAT'D YOU LEARN?

SPYDER WAS ALREADY AT THE BARN. I FOLLOWED SOME OF THEIR GUYS BACK TO A DIFFERENT FARM ON THE WESTERN SIDE OF THE CITY.
I *THINK* THE OTHER KIDS ARE BEING HELD IN THE MAIN HOUSE THERE. SPYDER HAD AN AWFUL LOT OF SECURITY SET UP AROUND IT.
WELL, LET'S GO SEE IT. WHERE TO?

LATER...

?
?
?

WHAT ON EARTH IS GOING ON HERE?
IT'S A CIVIL WAR BATTLE REENACTMENT.
THE BATTLE OF SECOND WINCHESTER, TO BE SPECIFIC. IT WAS ONE OF THE MAJOR BATTLES OF THE CIVIL WAR. THE CELEBRATIONS START TODAY AND GO ALL WEEKEND.

VERY CLEVER OF SPYDER. TOTAL CHAOS EVERYWHERE, WHICH MEANS A THOUSAND DISTRACTIONS TO TAKE ADVANTAGE OF. A HUNDRED CROWDS FOR THEM TO BLEND INTO.

BUT THEN IT'S EASIER FOR US TO BLEND IN TOO.
YES. I SUPPOSE IT IS.

RE-ENACTMENT
PARKING
$10
IT'S TEN BUCKS TO PARK.

ARE Y'ALL YANKEES, CONFEDERATES, OR IMPARTIAL OBSERVERS?
YANKEES, OF COURSE. IS THERE A SUTLER NEARBY?
NORTH END OF THE FIELD. THEY'LL FIX YOU UP REAL GOOD.

WHERE'S THE FARMHOUSE IN QUESTION?

LOOKS LIKE THAT'S BEHIND UNION LINES. WE'D BETTER DRESS ACCORDINGLY.

WELL, I HAPPEN TO BE HER GREAT-GREAT-GREAT-GRANDDAUGHTER. AND AS SUCH, THAT GIVES ME THE RIGHT TO FIGHT IN WHATEVER BATTLE I CHOOSE.

CYRUS HALE AND FAMILY, LOOKING TO JOIN YOUR FORCES SO THAT WE MAY AID IN RIDDING THE UNION OF CONFEDERATE SCOURGE.
THE THIRTY-FOURTH REGIMEN UNDER THE HONORABLE GENERAL ROBERT MILROY APPRECIATES YOUR HELP.
A FEW MINUTES LATER...
PAT PAT!

STATE YOUR BUSINESS.
I DON'T SUPPOSE ANY OF YOU KNOWS HOW TO WORK A CANNON? ONE OF OUR USUAL CANNONEERS CAME DOWN WITH DROPSY THIS MORNING.
I KNOW HOW TO WORK A CANNON. MY GRANDFATHER TAUGHT ME.

I FOUND ZOE. SECOND FLOOR, SOUTHERNMOST ROOM.

CHIP'S THERE TOO. AND JAWA.
LOOKS LIKE THEY'VE GOT THE WHOLE GANG. I COUNT SIX HOSTAGES.
AND MORE THAN TEN GUARDS. I'M GONNA GO A BIT CLOSER, DO SOME MORE INVASIVE RECON.

I SAID *I'M* GONNA GO.

MAKE SURE SHE LISTENS.

THERE'S TWO WALKIE-TALKIES IN THERE. I'VE GOT THE THIRD.

YOU DON'T SEEM THAT UPSET THAT HE LEFT YOU HERE.
GRANDPA'S ALWAYS RIGHT WHEN IT COMES TO THESE THINGS. HE WAS PROBABLY THE BEST SPY THE CIA EVER HAD UP UNTIL HIS RETIREMENT.

DOESN'T LOOK LIKE HE'S RETIRED TO ME.

NO, HE IS. HE STILL CONSULTS EVERY ONCE IN A WHILE, BUT HE'S NEVER AGREED TO BE ACTIVATED AGAIN UNTIL NOW.
REALLY? HE CERTAINLY SEEMS TO ENJOY IT.
OH, I KNOW HE DOES. BUT HE SAYS SPYING IS A YOUNG MAN'S GAME. AND THE LONGER YOU STAY IN, THE MORE ENEMIES YOU MAKE.

IT BECAME TOO DANGEROUS FOR HIM TO STAY ACTIVE. GRANDPA HAD TO GO UNDERGROUND YEARS AGO. I DON'T EVEN KNOW WHERE HE LIVES.
HOW OFTEN DO YOU GET TO SEE HIM?
EVERY MONTH OR SO. HE DROPS IN WHEN HE'S SURE THE COAST IS CLEAR. OF COURSE, I SUSPECT HE KEEPS TABS ON ME THE REST OF THE TIME.

OF COURSE HE KEEPS TABS ON YOU. YOU'RE HIS PRIDE AND JOY. THE PERFECT STUDENT THAT I NEVER WAS. NOTHING I DID WAS EVER GOOD ENOUGH.

HAS THE CIA EVER TRIED TO REACTIVATE YOUR GRANDFATHER BEFORE?

OH, SURE. THEY COME TO HIM ALL THE TIME.
SO WHY DID HE AGREE THIS TIME?

FOR A CHANCE TO ACTUALLY CONFRONT SPYDER.

NO. HE REACTIVATED BECAUSE OF *ME*.
I THINK SO. LIKE ALEXANDER SAID, YOU'RE CYRUS'S PRIDE AND JOY. HE KNEW YOU'D GOTTEN INVOLVED IN THIS AND HE WAS WORRIED ABOUT YOU.

TOOOT!
TO ARMS! JOHNNY REB PREPARES TO ATTACK! LET US MAKE THESE FIELDS RUN RED WITH HIS BLOOD!

THIS ISN'T ABOUT ME AT ALL. SPYDER NEVER WANTED ME.
THEY WANTED GRANDPA. THEY KNEW YOU'D COME TO ME FOR HELP, AND THAT IF I GOT INVOLVED, HE'D GET INVOLVED.

NO WAY. THEY COULDN'T BE THAT FAR AHEAD OF US.

THEY'RE ALWAYS THAT FAR AHEAD OF US.

THERE'S FEWER AGENTS ON HAND THAN I EXPECTED. AND THIS BATTLE IS DISTRACTING THEM. I'M GOING FOR THE HOSTAGES.

NO, GRANDPA! DON'T DO IT!

I HAVE TO. WE WON'T GET ANOTHER CHANCE LIKE THIS. I'LL BE IN AND OUT BEFORE THEY EVEN KNOW WHAT HIT THEM. GOING TO RADIO SILENCE.
WAIT! THEY KNOW YOU'RE COMING! THEY'VE WANTED YOU ALL ALONG!

CLICK!

HE'S TURNED OFF HIS RADIO. I'M GOING AFTER HIM.
ME TOO.

HEY! DON'T DESERT YOUR POSTS! THE BATTLE'S ABOUT TO BEGIN!

WHAT IS GOING ON HERE? THE CONFEDERACY IS ABOUT TO CHARGE US...
...AND YOU'RE LOLLING IN THE SUN LIKE AN OLD COON DOG! DO YOU NOT CARE A WHIT FOR YOUR COUNTRY?

I CARE MANY WITS FOR MY COUNTRY. IT'S JUST THAT SOMETHING VERY IMPORTANT IS HAPPENING.

THE BATTLE OF SECOND WINCHESTER IS HAPPENING, PRIVATE! YOU NEED TO LOAD THIS CANNON. THAT'S A DIRECT ORDER.

TOOOT!
BOOM!
BOOM!

COMMANDER RIPLEY, THIS IS THE ADVANCE PARTY. I HAVE REACHED THE DESTINATION...

...ALTHOUGH MY FATHER APPEARS TO HAVE GOTTEN LOST EN ROUTE.
DQ
MAP

I HAVE FAILED TO CONVENE WITH MY SUPERIOR, AS HE IS ALREADY IN PLACE TO ENGAGE THE ENEMY.
I INTEND TO EXTRACT HIM—AND THE OTHERS—BUT IT WON'T BE EASY. THERE ARE FAR MORE REBELS HERE THAN ORIGINALLY EXPECTED.
SO I NEED YOU TO CREATE A DIVERSION FOR ME.

UH, HOW SOON DO YOU NEED IT?
FAN!
SOMETIME IN THE NEXT TWO MINUTES WOULD BE NICE.

IS THAT A WALKIE-TALKIE? YOU CAN'T USE TWENTIETH-CENTURY TECHNOLOGY IN A CIVIL WAR BATTLE!

REST ASSURED, THOSE CONFEDERATES ARE CANNON FODDER.
PAT PAT!

SHAKE!

GUN POWDER

STUFF!

WUMPTH!

GRAB!
GUN

CRACK!

SHOVE!

THE LEAD CANNONEER SAYS YOU'VE LOST THE REST OF YOUR TEAM.
WE CAN TAKE IT FROM HERE, SON.

YOU MEN GOT HERE JUST IN TIME. I COULD REALLY USE SOME HELP TURNING THIS CANNON AROUND.

TURN THE CANNON? WHY? IT'S AIMED TOWARD THE BATTLE.

THE CONFEDERATES ARE PLANNING A SNEAK ATTACK BEHIND US. MY TEAM SPOTTED THEM RIGHT BEFORE THE BATTLE BEGAN.
BUT JOHNNY REB PICKED THEM OFF BEFORE WE COULD COUNTER.

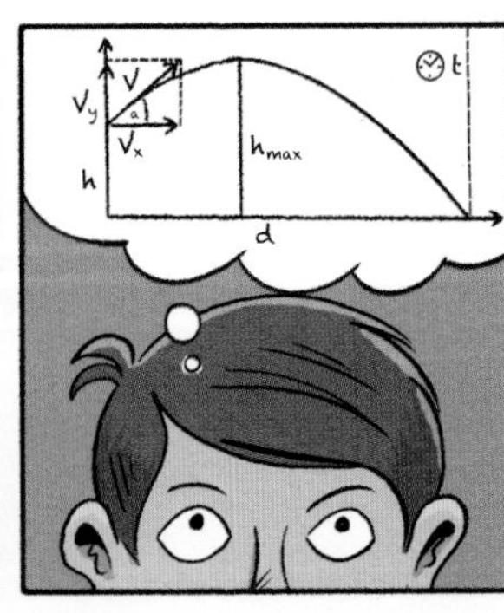

V
V_y
a
V_x
h
h_{max}
d
t

WHY HAS THIS CANNON BEEN TURNED AWAY FROM THE ENEMY?! WHAT IS THE MEANING OF THIS DISOBEDIENCE?

WE'RE COUNTERING A CONFEDERATE COMMANDO SNEAK ATTACK, SIR!

I DON'T SEE ANY COMMANDOS.
THEY WOULDN'T BE VERY GOOD COMMANDOS IF YOU COULD.

CRACKLE!

PACKAGE IS EN ROUTE.
BOOM!
WOOSH!!
UH-OH.
THWACK!

SIZZLE!

KABOOM!

FLIP!

BOOM!

WHAT HAVE YOU DONE?
WELL, IT'S OBVIOUS. WE'VE BLOWN UP A REBEL MINIVAN.

SWIPE!

WHACK!

CRACK!

THE CONFEDERACY DOESN'T DRIVE MINIVANS. THEY RIDE HORSES! YOU HAVE DESTROYED THE PROPERTY OF AN INNOCENT BYSTANDER!

SPIN!

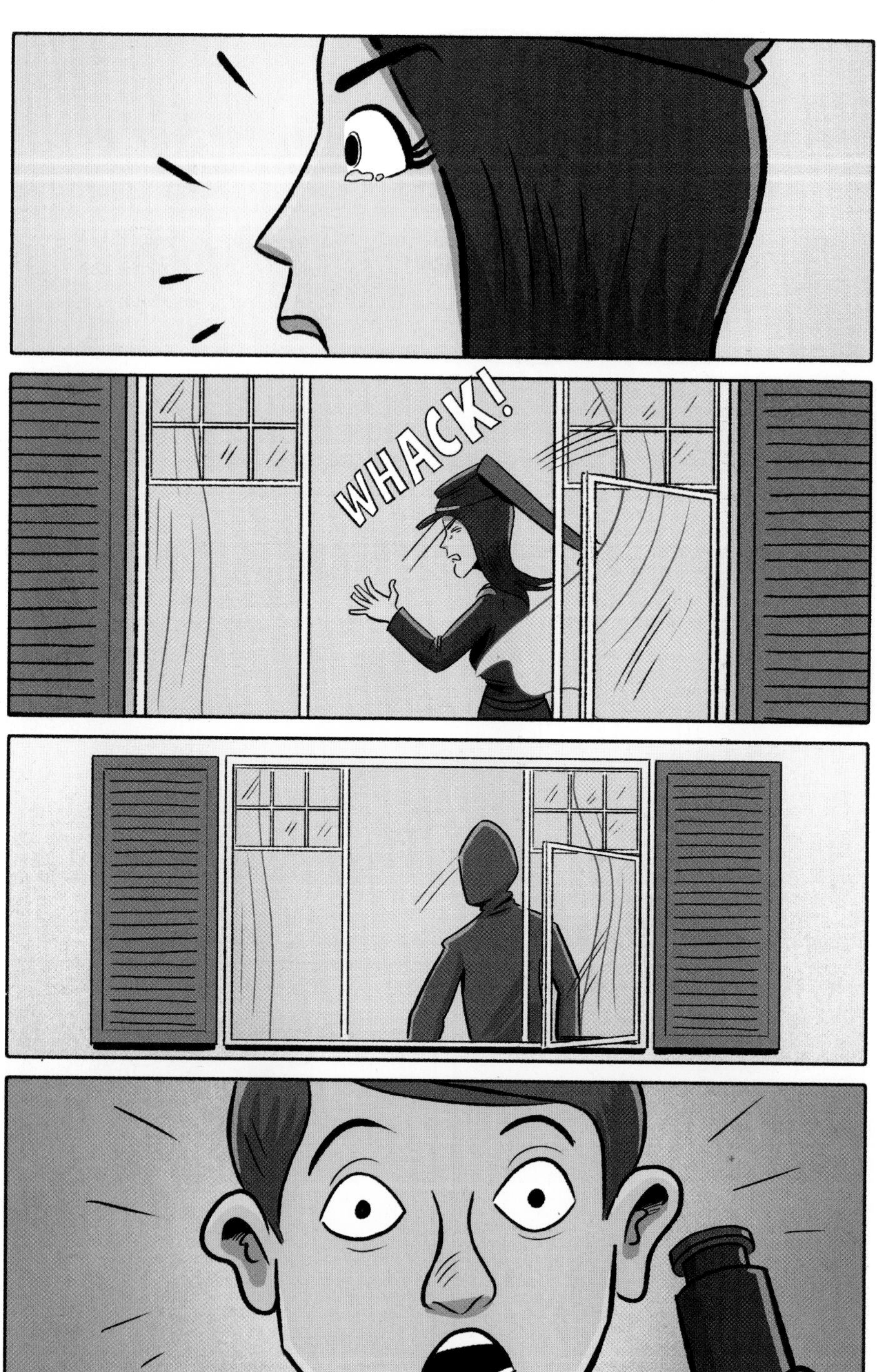
WHACK!

CYRUS! ERICA IS DOWN IN THE BEDROOM!

YOU'RE NOT GOING ANYWHERE–EXCEPT JAIL! I'M ARRESTING YOU FOR SEDITION!

OH MY GOSH! IS THAT GENERAL ULYSSES S. GRANT?

WHERE?

WOOSH!
OUCH.

LEAP!

WE'RE FREE! THANK YOU! THANK YOU!

ERICA'S STILL IN THERE! THEY GOT HER!

SKID!
SCREECH!

SKID!

WHAT HAPPENED? WHERE'S MY FAMILY?

ERICA AND CYRUS HAVE BEEN CAPTURED BY SPYDER.

WE NEED TO COMMANDEER A CAR AND GO AFTER THEM.

IT'S TOO LATE. WE'LL NEVER CATCH THEM.
WE WON'T IF WE DON'T TRY! WE NEED TO GET MOVING. NOW.

NO. FIRST, YOU NEED TO DEBRIEF US.

THERE'S NO TIME!
SPYDER ALREADY HAS TOO BIG OF A HEAD START. SO IF WE WANT TO RESCUE THE OTHERS, WE NEED TO FIGURE OUT WHERE THEY'RE HEADING.
AND THAT'S NOT GOING TO HAPPEN UNTIL YOU TELL US WHAT ON EARTH IS GOING ON.

OKAY. I BELIEVE THAT ALL OF THIS HAS BEEN A PLOT DEVISED BY SPYDER TO CAPTURE CYRUS HALE.
HOLD ON–I THOUGHT THEY WERE TRYING TO CAPTURE *YOU*.

NO. I WAS JUST A PAWN. THAT'S WHY THEY WERE SO OBVIOUS ABOUT COMING AFTER ME: SENDING ME NOTES, HAVING MURRAY HILL SHOW HIMSELF IN BROAD DAYLIGHT, DELIVERING A CONTRACT.
THEY KNEW I'D GO TO ERICA FOR HELP–AND THEY KNEW ERICA WOULDN'T PASS UP THE CHANCE TO PROVE HERSELF AGAINST SPYDER.
BUT WHAT DOES THAT HAVE TO DO WITH CYRUS?

I THINK SPYDER WANTED THE CIA TO FREAK OUT A LITTLE, TOO. THE AGENCY SENT ALEXANDER HALE TO KEEP AN EYE ON ME. AND THEN ASKED CYRUS TO REACTIVATE—WHICH HE DID TO PROTECT HIS FAMILY.
ERICA IS THE ONLY PERSON CYRUS WOULD COME OUT OF RETIREMENT TO HELP. AND THEN THEY COULD CAPTURE HIM.

THE QUESTION IS, *WHY* DID SPYDER WANT CYRUS HALE SO BADLY?

THEY HEADED NORTH, BUT THERE ARE TEN THOUSAND PLACES THEY COULD BE ALREADY.
HOW DO WE NARROW DOWN WHERE THEY'VE GONE?
SHOULDN'T WE NOTIFY THE AGENCY?
WE CAN'T. ACCORDING TO THE HALES, THE CIA'S FULL OF DOUBLE AGENTS FOR SPYDER. WE CAN'T TRUST ANYONE THERE.
CHOCO POPS

FOR NOW, THE ONLY AGENT WE CAN TRUST IS ALEXANDER. HE OUGHT TO BE TEAM LEADER.

NOD
NOD
NOD
NOD
NOD
?

SO, CAN YOU GO FIND OUT WHAT HE'S COME UP WITH?

ALEXANDER, WE NEED YOUR HELP.
NO YOU DON'T. MY HELP IS THE *LAST* THING ANYONE NEEDS RIGHT NOW.

THAT'S NOT TRUE. NONE OF US HAS ANY IDEA WHY SPYDER EVEN WANTED TO CAPTURE YOUR FATHER.

WELL, NEITHER DO I. DAD WAS RIGHT. I'M A FAILURE. A DISGRACE TO THE HALE FAMILY NAME.
SO YOU'RE NOT GOING TO HELP US RESCUE HIM? BECAUSE HE WAS TOUGH ON YOU?

NO, I'M NOT GOING TO HELP BECAUSE *I'M A BAD SPY*. HOW AM I SUPPOSED TO PULL OFF A RESCUE?
I'M A SHAM. A FAKE. A CHARLATAN. MY ENTIRE CAREER HAS BEEN BUILT ON LIES.

THAT CAN'T BE TRUE. YOU COULDN'T POSSIBLY HAVE THE REPUTATION YOU DO WITHOUT SOME TALENTS.

PERHAPS.

THERE ARE SIX STUDENTS IN THERE WILLING TO DO WHATEVER IT TAKES. BUT THEY DON'T KNOW WHERE TO BEGIN. THEY NEED SOMETHING TO BELIEVE IN RIGHT NOW, AND WHAT THEY BELIEVE IN IS *YOU.*
SO ARE YOU GOING TO WALLOW IN SELF-PITY OR ARE YOU ACTUALLY GOING TO DO SOMETHING?

WHAT DO YOU NEED ME TO DO?

BE ALEXANDER HALE. NOT THE *REAL* ALEXANDER HALE. JUST THE ALEXANDER HALE EVERYONE *THINKS* IS REAL.

PAT
PAT!

IT IS AN HONOR TO HAVE THE CHANCE TO SERVE UNDER YOU, AGENT HALE.

AND IT IS MY HONOR TO SERVE WITH SUCH A FINE-LOOKING TROOP OF STUDENTS.

SO, WHAT'S YOUR PLAN?

WELL, THIS MAY SOUND A BIT UNORTHODOX, BUT...

...SOMETIMES THE BEST WAY TO FIGURE SOMETHING OUT IS TO SEE IF SOMEONE ELSE HAS ALREADY FIGURED IT OUT BEFORE YOU.

YOU MEAN LIKE COPYING SOMEONE'S HOMEWORK?

IN A WAY. ONLY, IN REAL LIFE, THAT'S NOT ALWAYS SUCH A BAD THING. WHY SHOULD WE WASTE TIME TRYING TO FIGURE OUT WHERE SPYDER HAS TAKEN MY FAMILY IF SOMEONE ELSE HAS ALREADY DONE THE LEGWORK? NOW, DOES ANYONE ELSE KNOW WHERE SPYDER'S HIDEOUT IS?

I THINK SOMEONE MIGHT.

WHAT DO YOU MEAN?

WHEN I GOT THE FIRST NOTE FROM SPYDER, ERICA FOUND AN EXTREMELY TINY PIECE OF GRIT ON IT. SHE THOUGHT IT MIGHT BE A LEAD TO WHERE THE LETTER HAD BEEN WRITTEN AND WAS GOING TO GET SOMEONE TO ANALYZE IT FOR HER.

WHO?

I DON'T KNOW.

PROBABLY CHESTER SNODGRASS. HE'S A FORENSIC GEOLOGIST IN THE DEPARTMENT OF EVIDENCE ASSESSMENT.

CAN YOU CALL HIM?
UNFORTUNATELY, NO. CHESTER IS ON VACATION THIS WEEK AND I LOST ALL HIS CONTACT INFORMATION ALONG WITH MY PHONE IN THE RIVER.

WELL, WE WOULDN'T HAVE TO TALK TO CHESTER DIRECTLY. IT'S STANDARD PROCEDURE TO LOG ALL EVIDENCE ANALYSIS ON THE CIA CENTRAL COMPUTER SYSTEM.
WE SIMPLY NEED ACCESS TO IT.
CAN YOU DO IT REMOTELY? THERE'S A COMPUTER IN THE HOUSE.

IT'S NOT THAT SIMPLE. FOR SECURITY REASONS, YOU CAN'T ACCESS THE CENTRAL SYSTEM WITH MERELY ANY DEVICE.

SO WE JUST NEED TO CALL SOMEONE AT THE CIA AND HAVE THEM ACCESS THE SYSTEM FOR US.

DONK!

DID YOU FORGET ALREADY? THE CIA IS CRAWLING WITH DOUBLE AGENTS.
BUT NOT EVERYONE IS SUSPECT.
IF YOU WANT TO FIGURE OUT WHO'S DEFINITELY NOT WORKING FOR SPYDER, YOU SIMPLY LOOK FOR SOMEONE WHOSE CAREER SPYDER HAS RUINED.

TINA CUEVO.

OKAY, I GOT IT! GIVE ME A FEW MOMENTS. IT'S A LONG REPORT. WOW. WHO EVER KNEW YOU COULD TELL SO MUCH FROM ONE PIECE OF GRIT? AH, HERE WE GO. IT'S A PIECE OF COAL.
TAP TAP TAP!

THAT'S IT? I ALREADY KNEW IT WAS COAL.

SEEMS LIKE EVERY VEIN OF COAL IS DIFFERENT. SLIGHT ALTERATIONS IN THE VARIOUS ELEMENTS AND SUCH. THIS BIT OF COAL CAME FROM A SEAM IN EITHER VLADIVOSTOK, RUSSIA...

UGH.

OR THE JUNCTION MINE, NEAR SHEPHERDSTOWN, WEST VIRGINIA.

HOW FAR IS THAT FROM WINCHESTER, VIRGINIA?

ONLY ABOUT THIRTY MILES.

THAT SOUNDS LIKE THE PLACE. DO YOU HAVE COORDINATES?

CLATTER!
EMERGENCY FLARE
20
AUTO HIRE
Walmart

THAT'S IT? IT DOESN'T LOOK LIKE MUCH.
DON'T BE SUCH A FLEMING. THIS IS A TEMPORARY HIDEOUT, NOT THEIR WORLD HEADQUARTERS.
BESIDES, THE *REAL* CENTER OF OPERATIONS IS PROBABLY INSIDE THE MINE. LOOK.

SPLOSH!

DIP!

JUST GET BEHIND YOUR TARGET AND CLAP THIS OVER THEIR NOSE AND MOUTH.

WHAT IS IT?
SNIFF SNIFF!

SIGH!
SLAM!

KNOCKOUT DROPS. AND AS YOU CAN ALL SEE, THEY WORK FAST. SO BE CAREFUL.

ОВЕРХНОСТНАЯ КЕТА
СИСТЕМА КОНТРОЛЯ

CAN ANYONE HERE READ RUSSIAN?

THE METAL CASE RIGHT BESIDE THE WINNEBAGO.
I SEE IT. IT SAYS: "EXTERIOR MONKEY MONITORING SYSTEM."
NO. IT SAYS "SURFACE MISSILE CONTROL SYSTEM."

OH. I MUST HAVE BEEN USING THE WRONG DIALECT.

SPYDER HAS A MISSILE?

WE SHOULD HAVE KNOWN THEY'D HAVE MORE. THEY ALREADY FIRED ONE AT US, TWO DAYS AGO...

WHAT IS IT?

ALEXANDER, EARLIER TODAY, YOUR FATHER SAID THAT THE GLOBAL POSITIONING SYSTEM ISN'T AS ACCURATE AS EVERYONE THINKS.
WHAT DID HE MEAN BY THAT?

SO *THAT'S* WHAT THEY WANT WITH HIM.

WHAT DO YOU MEAN?

THE GLOBAL POSITIONING SYSTEM WAS DEVELOPED BY THE DEPARTMENT OF DEFENSE IN THE 1970S.

MY FATHER WAS THE CIA LIAISON TO THE PROJECT. THE ORIGINAL PURPOSE OF GPS HAD NOTHING TO DO WITH GIVING EVERYONE DIRECTIONS IN THEIR CARS. IT WAS FOR THE MILITARY.
MISSILE GUIDANCE SYSTEMS.
AMONG OTHER THINGS. MY FATHER KNEW ALL ALONG THAT THE MILITARY WOULD NEVER BE ABLE TO KEEP GPS UNDER TIGHT WRAPS. EVENTUALLY, THE PUBLIC WOULD BE ABLE TO USE IT.

MY FATHER FELT THAT WOULD BE A SECURITY RISK, SO HE CONVINCED DEFENSE TO PURPOSELY BUILD ERRORS INTO THE SYSTEM...

...TO PROTECT CERTAIN LOCATIONS THAT MIGHT BE TARGETED BY TERRORISTS.

BUT YOUR FATHER KNOWS THE ACTUAL COORDINATES FOR THOSE PLACES?
YES. HE FELT IT WAS TOO DANGEROUS TO RECORD THEM ANYWHERE. SO HE MEMORIZED THEM.

BUT NOW, SPYDER CAN MAKE HIM GIVE THEM UP.

I'M AFRAID SO. IF THEY HAD ONLY CAPTURED MY FATHER, HE'D NEVER GIVE UP THE INFORMATION.

BUT SPYDER MUST HAVE KNOWN THAT, BECAUSE THEY CAPTURED ERICA, TOO.
SHE'S MY FATHER'S ONLY WEAKNESS. HE'D DO ANYTHING TO PROTECT HER.

IT LOOKS LIKE THEY'VE GOT A RUSSIAN OMSK-CLASS SURFACE-TO-SURFACE MISSILE HERE. IT'S BIG ENOUGH TO LEVEL THE WHITE HOUSE.
BUT THE OMSK IS AN OLD MISSILE. WE'RE TALKING EARLY COLD WAR. DESPITE THE LARGE PAYLOAD, ITS RANGE IS LIMITED. LESS THAN THIRTY MILES.

WASHINGTON, DC, IS TOO FAR, THEN.

BUT CAMP DAVID ISN'T!

THE COUNTRY RESIDENCE FOR THE PRESIDENT OF THE UNITED STATES? THAT'S NEAR HERE?
YES. DOES ANYONE KNOW IF THE PRESIDENT IS THERE RIGHT NOW?
HE IS. HE'S HOSTING THE BRITISH PRIME MINISTER AND A FEW OTHER EUROPEAN LEADERS.

THE PERFECT SET OF TARGETS FOR AN EVIL ORGANIZATION WITH A STOLEN MISSILE.
LOOKS LIKE WE GOT HERE JUST IN TIME.
ASSUMING WE CAN ACTUALLY STOP THEM.

YES. IT'D BE VERY NICE IF WE COULD DO THAT.
BEEP!

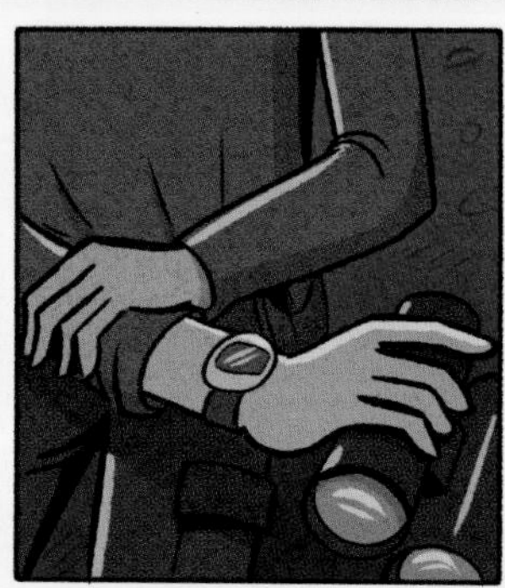

THUMP!
THUMP!

STEP ONE'S A SUCCESS.

PLOP!

NOW THAT EVERYONE'S UP TO SPEED, WE NEED TO FIGURE OUT OUR NEXT MOVE. WHO HERE IS THE MOST QUALIFIED TO REPROGRAM THE MISSILE CONTROL SYSTEM?
I THINK *YOU* ARE.

ME?

YES. ACCORDING TO YOUR FILES, YOU'VE REPROGRAMMED THE CONTROL SYSTEM OF A MISSILE TWICE. ONCE WITH ONLY TWENTY-THREE SECONDS TO LAUNCH.

AH. SO I HAVE. DOES ANYONE ELSE KNOW HOW TO DO THIS? AS AN EMERGENCY BACKUP, IN CASE SOMETHING SHOULD HAPPEN TO ME?

LOOKS LIKE YOU'LL HAVE TO HANDLE IT, AGENT HALE. TAKE BEN WITH YOU. HE'S THE MATH GENIUS, SO HE CAN HELP YOU WITH ANY CALCULATIONS.
THE REST OF US WILL RESCUE CYRUS AND ERICA.

LET'S MOVE.
CLICK!

HAVE YOU EVER ACTUALLY REPROGRAMMED THE CONTROL SYSTEM FOR A MISSILE?
UH...NO. IN ONE CASE, A FELLOW SPY NAMED KEN PARKER DID THE REPROGRAMMING, BUT THEN HE WHACKED HIS HEAD DURING THE ESCAPE AND GOT AMNESIA, SO I TOOK THE CREDIT.

AND THE OTHER TIME?

THE MISSILE JUST BLEW UP ON THE LAUNCHPAD. PROBABLY AN ERROR IN CONSTRUCTION. LUCKY BREAK, REALLY.

SO YOU HAVE NO IDEA HOW TO STOP THE MISSILE FROM LAUNCHING?
NO. BUT THEN, I DON'T REALLY HAVE ANY IDEA HOW TO RESCUE MY FATHER AND DAUGHTER, EITHER. SO IT'S KIND OF A RELIEF THAT SOMEONE ELSE IS HANDLING THAT.

SHHH! ENEMY AHEAD. LIGHTS OFF.

I'M SORRY. HE'S MY FATHER. I CAN'T LEAVE SAVING HIM TO A BUNCH OF KIDS.

WAIT! YOU CAN'T JUST LEAVE ME...

NOW WHAT AM I SUPPOSED TO DO?

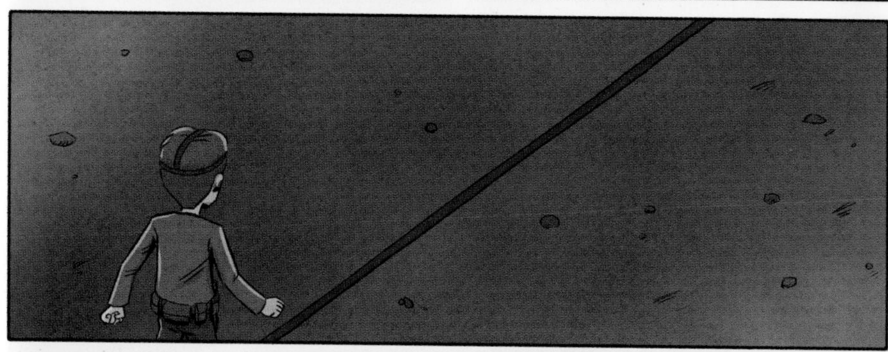

4:29
CRUNCH
CRUNCH!

HANDS UP. THEN BACK AWAY FROM THE DESK.
CRUNCH!
CRUNCHY CHUNKS

HOLY COW. YOU FOUND US.
CRU CHUN

I *KNEW* YOU WERE GOOD.

SHUT DOWN THE MISSILE, MURRAY.

I'D LOVE TO, BEN. REALLY. BUT I CAN'T.

DON'T LIE TO ME. YOU'LL BE SORRY.

I'M NOT LYING. I REALLY CAN'T SHUT THIS THING DOWN. FOR TWO REASONS: FIRST, I DON'T KNOW HOW TO.
AND THE SECOND REASON?
MY BOSS IS RIGHT BEHIND YOU.

I KNOW BETTER THAN TO TRUST ANYTHING THAT COMES OUT OF YOUR MOUTH.

USUALLY A WISE POLICY. ONLY THIS TIME, HE ACTUALLY HAPPENS TO BE TELLING THE TRUTH.

JOSHUA HALLAL, I PRESUME?

WOW, RIPLEY. YOU FIGURED THAT ONE OUT TOO?

I'LL TAKE UP
THE REAR.

FLUSH!

HEY! WHAT DO YOU THINK YOU'RE DOING HERE?!

RUN!

RATS!
YOU'RE NOT GOING ANYWHERE.

YOU GUYS REALLY THOUGHT YOU COULD GET US WITH A SNEAK ATTACK? NOT A CHANCE.

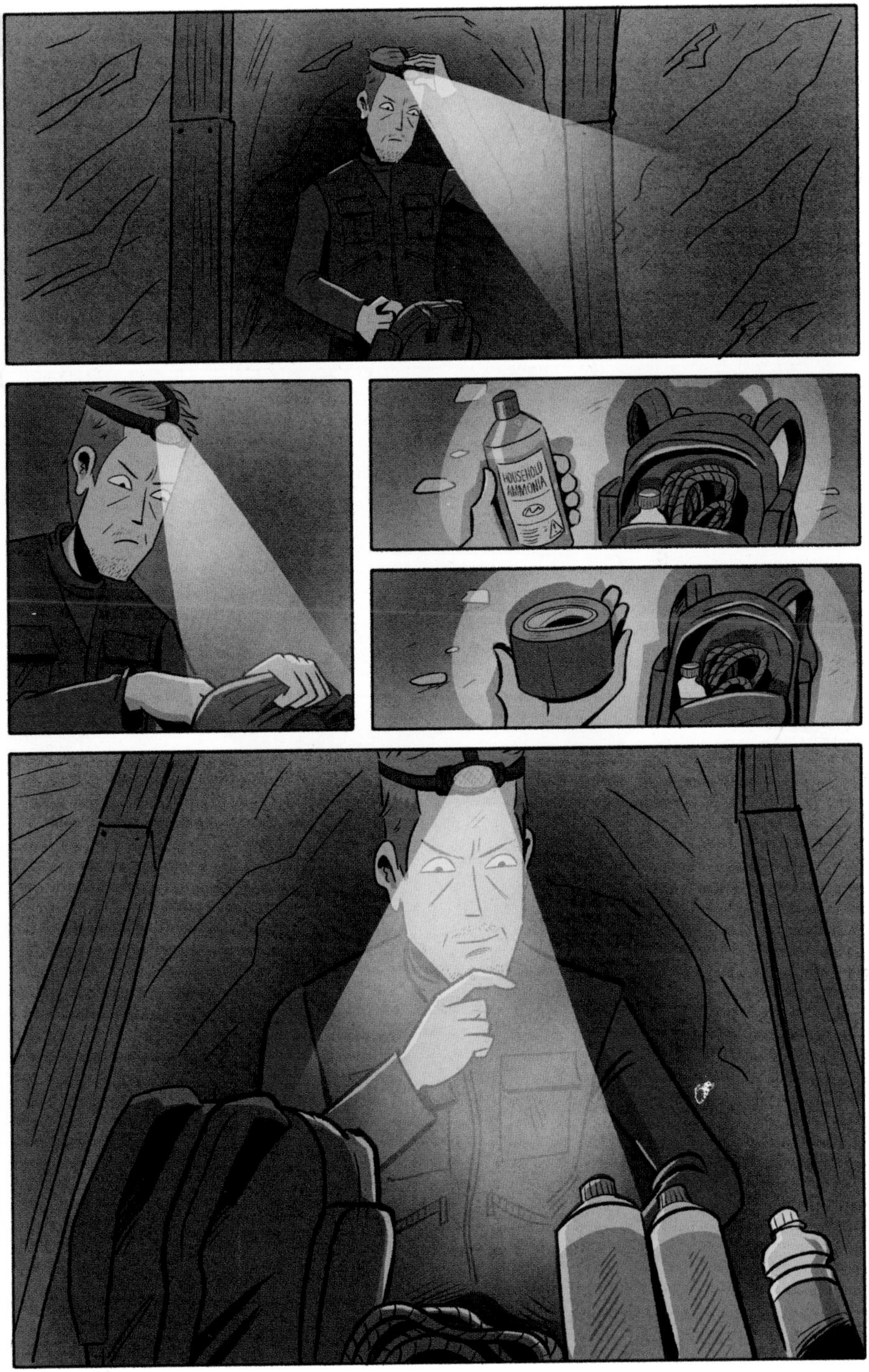

HOUSEHOLD
AMMONIA

DROP YOUR WEAPONS.

3:05
HOW DID YOU KNOW IT WAS ME?

THE WHOLE TIME WE'VE BEEN UP AGAINST YOU, EVERYONE ASSUMED WE HAD ANOTHER MOLE INSIDE THE SCHOOL. BUT WHOEVER IT WAS OBVIOUSLY KNEW FAR MORE THAN MOST STUDENTS.
THEY'D HAVE TO KNOW SPY SCHOOL AND SPY CAMP AS WELL AS ERICA—AND SHE LEARNED A LOT OF THAT INFORMATION FROM YOU.

SO IT OCCURRED TO ME, IF SPYDER COULD DELIVER SOMEONE WHO WASN'T MURRAY TO APPLE VALLEY WITHOUT ANYONE NOTICING, THEY COULD EASILY HAVE HELPED YOU FAKE YOUR OWN DEATH.
THAT'S SOME NICE DEDUCTIVE WORK.

SEE? I TOLD YOU BEN WAS SMART. EVERYONE HERE RAZZED ME FOR LETTING HIM DEFEAT OPERATION SCORPIO, BUT NOW HE'S FIGURED OUT YOUR GENIUS PLAN, TOO.
WHAT DO YOU SAY, BEN? ARE YOU GOING TO SIGN THAT CONTRACT OR WHAT?

THAT WASN'T JUST A RUSE TO LURE CYRUS HALE OUT OF RETIREMENT?

IT WAS DESIGNED TO DO BOTH: GRAB YOUR ATTENTION AND GET THE WHOLE HALE FAMILY INVOLVED.

YOU'RE REALLY OFFERING ME A JOB AGAIN?

MY SUPERIORS STILL THINK YOU HAVE POTENTIAL. HOWEVER, THIS IS THE LAST TIME WE'LL BE ABLE TO MAKE YOU AN OFFER.

YOU'RE EITHER WITH US OR AGAINST US.

POKE!

1:13

I DIDN'T FINISH TELLING YOU HOW I KNEW YOU WERE STILL ALIVE. I WAS WATCHING ERICA WHEN YOU CAPTURED HER. I DIDN'T SEE YOU, BUT I SAW HER FACE.
I'VE NEVER SEEN HER SO SURPRISED BEFORE. IT WAS AS THOUGH SHE WAS SEEING SOMEONE WHO'D COME BACK FROM THE DEAD. BUT I REALIZE NOW THAT THERE WAS SOMETHING MORE TO IT.

WHAT?

BETRAYAL. YOU WERE THE ONLY OTHER STUDENT THAT ERICA ADMIRED. SHE BELIEVED IN YOU, JOSHUA. SHE THOUGHT YOU STOOD FOR THE SAME THINGS SHE DID.
AND NOW, YOU'RE PLANNING TO KILL OFF THE PRESIDENT AND A DOZEN HEADS OF STATE AT ONCE.

YOU FIGURED THAT OUT TOO?

IT'S PATHETIC, REALLY. IF YOU REALLY CARED ABOUT ANYTHING, YOU'D USE YOUR POWER TO EFFECT SOME CHANGE.
BUT ASSASSINATION? THAT'S THE SPINELESS WAY OUT. IT'S EASY TO PULL A TRIGGER OR PUSH A LAUNCH BUTTON. ANY MORON CAN DO IT.

SPYDER DOES NOT HIRE MORONS. DO YOU THINK A MORON COULD HAVE CONCOCTED THIS PLAN? OR BENT THE CIA TO THEIR WILL?

OR OBTAINED AND INSTALLED THAT?

SWISH!
KRING!
0:05

PLOP!
0:01
ROOOAAR!

LAUNCH IN PROGRESS
ROOOOAAAR!
CLICK!

WHAT DID YOU DO?

I THINK I JUST THWARTED YOUR PLANS.

TAP! TAP! TAP!
CRUNCHY CHUNKS

UNBELIEVABLE! BEN, YOU *HAVE* TO START WORKING WITH US.

NO. THE CONTRACT'S RESCINDED. YOU'RE TOO MUCH LIKE ERICA.
WE COULD NEVER TRUST YOU TO DO THE WRONG THING.

SPUTTER!
CRUNCH!
CRASH!
BOOM!

WOOSH!
VWUMPH!
SLAM!
CRASH!
SLAM!

RUMBLE RUMB
DONK!
RUMBLE RUMBLE RU
RUMBLE RUMBLE RU

HEY, YOU! GET BACK HERE!

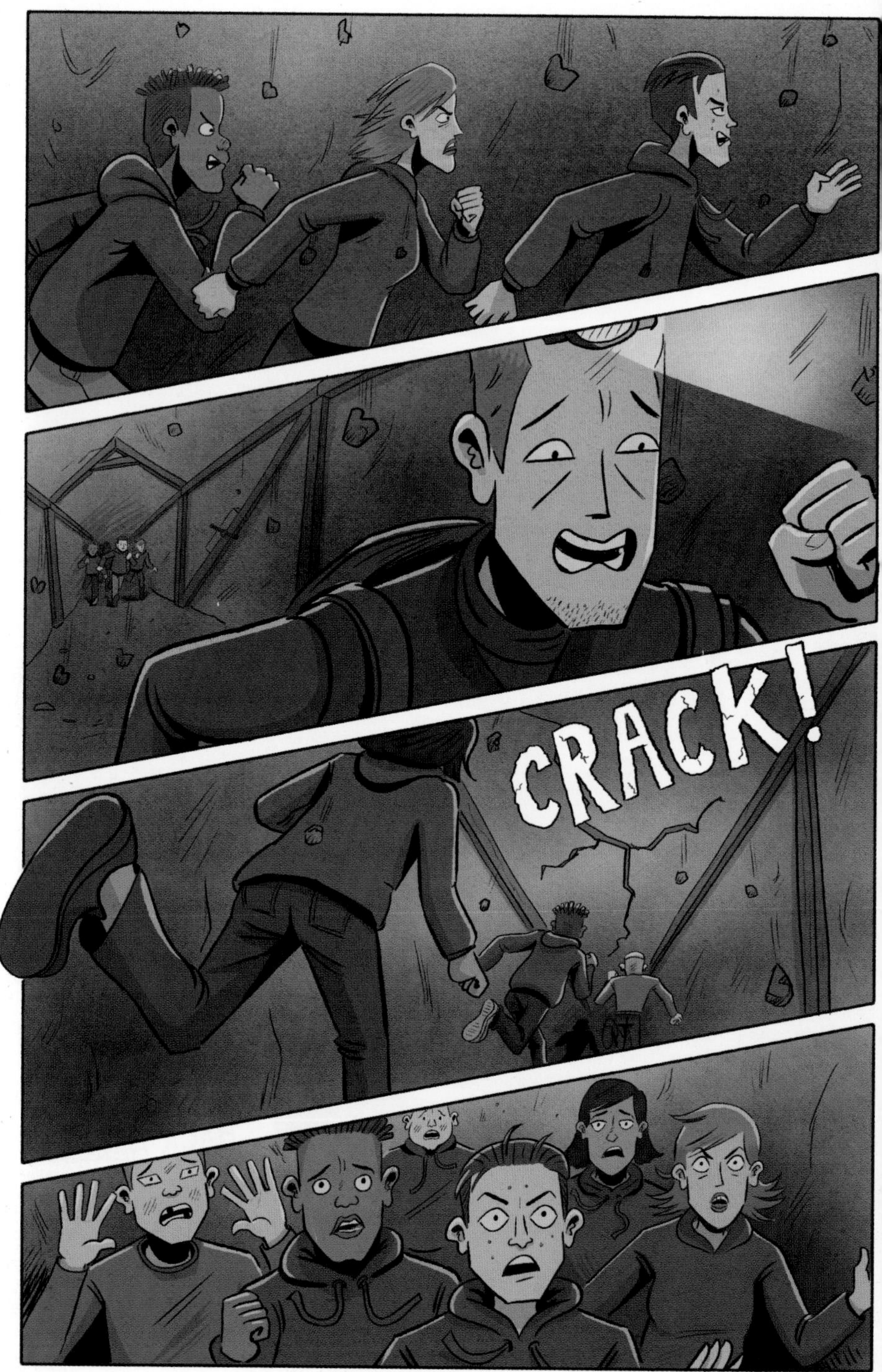
CRACK!

CRASH!

SPIN!

ARRGH

HOP!
URGH!
SKIP!

DAD?!

THANK YOU, SIR! WE KNEW WE COULD COUNT ON YOU!

OH, IT WAS NOTHING. JUST YOUR STANDARD "SIX VERSUS ONE" HAND-TO-HAND COMBAT TUNNEL MATCH—I DID SOMETHING SIMILAR YEARS AGO IN A HOSTAGE RESCUE MISSION IN BULGARIA...

WITH ALL DUE RESPECT, AGENT HALE, WE'VE GOTTA GET OUT OF HERE!

SKID!
THEY'RE OKAY! GET THE BAD GUYS!
THE MISSILES ARE GOING TO BLOW! GET EVERYONE AND CLEAR THE MINE NOW!

IT'S NOT GONNA HAPPEN.
LAST CHANCE, BEN. I CAN STILL GET YOU A LUCRATIVE JOB AT SPYDER. LET ME GO AND I'LL MAKE IT WORTH YOUR WHILE.
DUFF!

BLAM!
BLAM!
BLAM!

WARREN!

SORRY!

WHERE'D THE FIRST GUY GO?
GUURGH.

IT'S HARD TO RUN AWAY WHEN YOU DON'T HAVE THE KEYS!

ZOE! CAN YOU HANDLE MURRAY FOR ME?

GLAD TO.
DUFF!
THAT'S FOR BETRAYING YOUR FRIENDS!
OOOF!

GET EVERYONE OUT OF HERE BEFORE THE MINE BLOWS.
TOSS!

WHAT ABOUT YOU?

I'LL BE OKAY... I THINK.

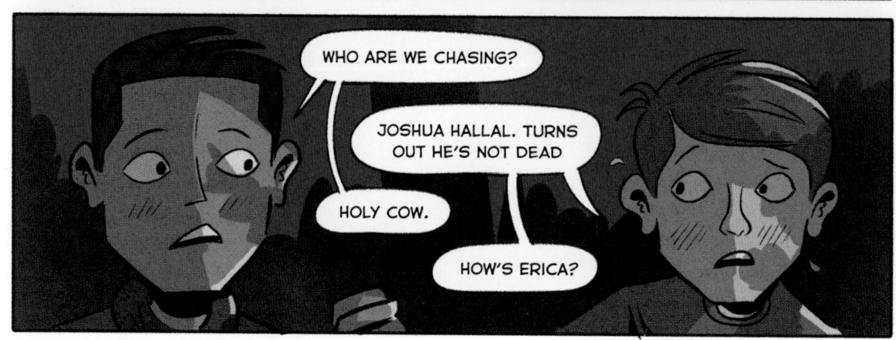
WHO ARE WE CHASING?
JOSHUA HALLAL. TURNS OUT HE'S NOT DEAD
HOLY COW.
HOW'S ERICA?

SHE'LL BE ALL RIGHT. THANKS TO ALEXANDER. THE REST OF US RAN RIGHT INTO A TRAP. LUCKILY, ALEXANDER SAVED US.
ALEXANDER?! REALLY?
WHY DO YOU SOUND SO SURPRISED? THIS IS ALEXANDER HALE WE'RE TALKING ABOUT.

SCREEECH!!

BURST!

WHOOOA!

SCREECH!

THERE'S NO OTHER BUCKETS HERE. HE'S GOING TO GET AWAY.
BO

OM!
CRRACK!

VWUMPH!

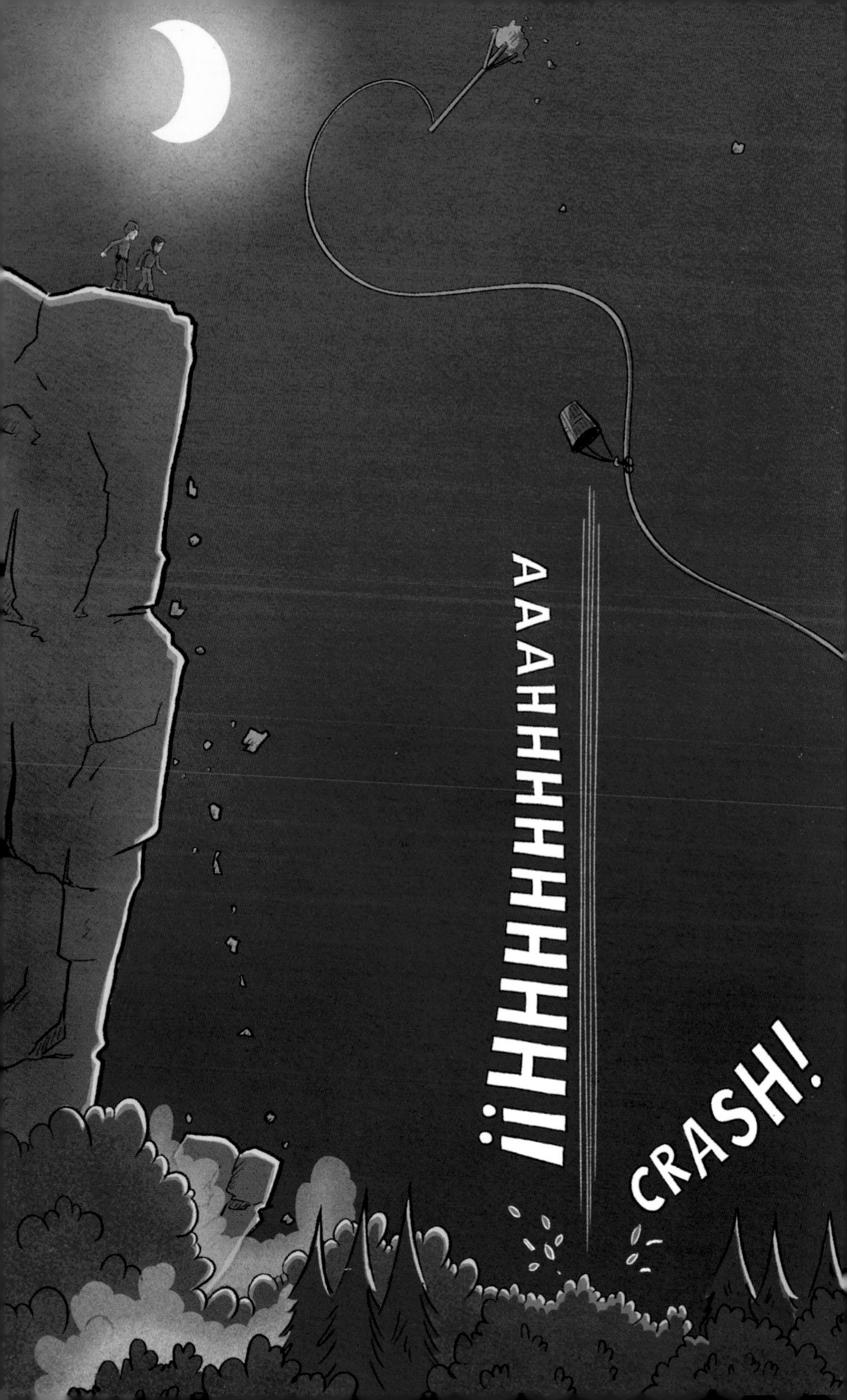

AAAHHHHHHHHH!!

CRASH!

THIS TIME, I DON'T THINK HE'S FAKING HIS DEATH.

NICE WORK.
LIMP LIMP!

THANKS. SHOULDN'T YOU BE RECUPERATING RIGHT NOW?
PROBABLY. BUT I COULDN'T EXACTLY SIT STILL WHILE JOSHUA WAS ON THE LOOSE. NOT AFTER WHAT HE DID TO ME.

DON'T WORRY. MURRAY'S TIED UP NICE AND TIGHT.

WHERE'S THE BAD GUY?

YOU YANKS DON'T LIKE TO TAKE ANYONE OUT THE EASY WAY, DO YOU?

ARE YOU TWO A COUPLE NOW?

THEY'VE BEEN EVER SINCE LONDON.
HOW DID *YOU* KNOW? WE WERE TRYING TO KEEP IT A SECRET.

WHAT HAPPENED?

BAD GUY'S GONE. BEN AND JAWA GOT HIM.

YOU KIDS HAVE ALL DONE THE WORLD A GREAT SERVICE THIS EVENING.

AND I MEAN *ALL* OF YOU.

BUT ENOUGH SELF-CONGRATULATION.
THIS JOSHUA HALLAL CHARACTER WAS FAR TOO YOUNG, WHICH MEANS THAT WHOEVER'S RUNNING THE SHOW IS STILL AT LARGE...

...AND AS LONG AS THEY'RE OUT THERE, THEY'RE GOING TO BE TROUBLE.

SO COME ON, KIDS. WE'VE STILL GOT PLENTY OF WORK CUT OUT FOR US.

I OWE YOU MY LIFE, RIPLEY.

NO. YOU OWE YOUR FATHER.

WHO WOULD HAVE NEVER FOUND US IF IT WASN'T FOR YOU. AND HE CERTAINLY WOULDN'T HAVE FIGURED OUT HOW TO STOP THOSE MISSILES, EITHER.
IN FACT, I'M NOT SURE *I* COULD HAVE STOPPED THEM. HOW DID YOU DO IT?

I JUST UNPLUGGED THE SYSTEM.

RIPLEY, YOU'RE ONE OF A KIND.
BY THE WAY, HAPPY BIRTHDAY.

THANKS.

I DIDN'T EXACTLY HAVE TIME TO SHOP, GIVEN THE KIDNAPPING AND ALL, SO I GOT YOU THIS.

IS THIS MURRAY'S?

I TOLD HIM THAT IF SPYDER EVER MESSES WITH YOU AGAIN, HE'S GONNA LOSE A LOT MORE THAN THAT.

THANKS.

COULD YOU GIVE ME A LITTLE HELP GETTING BACK?
OF COURSE. I'M ALWAYS HERE FOR YOU.

AND I'LL ALWAYS BE HERE FOR YOU, RIPLEY.